JERMAIN L. REEVES

GALAXY GOODFELLOW

Magical Thinker

I see you, Mister Tree
Standing there, in the silence of certainty
Away from their make-believe garden
They're not hanging anyone from you today
So, you're as beautiful as the rainbow miles above you

PART I

Mansaville:
City of the Tiger

1

That cute little dark-skinned boy almost passed out when he saw the devil. He got to running out of that house so fast, nothing could've caught him. The devil's other name was Old Scratch. Funny enough, since he didn't look old, and he had never scratched anybody—at least not they skin. He only cut your soul, and Galaxy knew it better than other folks 'cause he was the only one who could see Old Scratch . . . well, at least right now. A few people could see the devil paddling his raft on the Confederate River, but everyone felt him. They never felt his touch, but they sho' felt his evil deeds.

He's been known to stab people to death. The crazy thing is, he can kill somebody with his knife and put a spell on the dead body. It can make the body act like it's still alive. It can walk and talk for three days! And looking at it, you wouldn't be able to tell. Not everybody knowed about the dead bodies that could speak like the living—not even that cute little boy that just saw Old Scratch.

The boy's name was Galaxy Goodfellow. Lord knows, he was a pretty little fella. His skin looked like dark chocolate. Barely had any marks on it. He had that shiny, curly black hair like them folks from the islands, except he was from here—right here in South Carolina—and he wasn't even mixed with nothing. Both his parents were just as black as midnight. And he had some of the whitest teeth. His smile made them little girls melt like custard, and some men too. Those poor girls didn't know he wasn't studying about them. He didn't bitmo want to get in bed with a girl. He only liked men—them rough ones, too. He wanted men to give him some of that "good-good." It just tickled me to death 'cause that "good-good" is what can get you into a heap of trouble.

Everyone in the room liked to fell on the floor when Galaxy was born. It was something chilly outside that day when Maxine caught a ride with her neighbor to get to the hospital. Them 'tractions in her belly told her the baby was a-coming. And Lord knows, he did. Time they got her in the bed, little Galaxy was fighting to get out. They barely had time to hook her up to the medicine machines. Poor Maxine did the best she could, bless her heart. The doctor kept telling her to push harder, and she finally got the strength to do it.

Galaxy's head poked out first. The rest of his little body came out next. They knew Galaxy was all right 'cause he was justa crying. Couldn't get him to shut up. That got a chuckle out of the doctor and the nurse. Even Maxine smiled.

Her husband wasn't there, so the doctor cut the cord. The nurse wiped him up and handed him to his momma. Maxine was crying tears of joy. She had run out of them bad tears. Her world had done changed now that she was a momma, but it was 'bout to change some more. They all looked at Galaxy. They were smiling like Cheshire cats until they seen the scariest sight. Baby Galaxy had fire coming out of his hands! A bright blue ball of it. Big enough so everyone could see it, but small enough for them to pretend they didn't.

The first sound Galaxy heard from his mother was a scream. The nurse hollered too. The doctor held it together. Ain't none of them speak a word about it. They shoulda just talked it out, but they chose to tuck it away in they minds. That's what started they struggles. They didn't want to talk about it, so they did one of the worst things black folks do.

They carried on.

2

You just heard from Grandma Sarah, a wise woman who was speaking to you from heaven. In this tale, you will meet many others, including the devil himself. Though there is some romance, this is not a love story. It is a Southern Gothic family saga full of many narratives that will frighten you, disgust you, and perhaps even turn you on. You are not obligated to like it. You are only required to suspend your disbelief and submit to the supernatural.

Be that as it may, Grandma Sarah was right. Galaxy Goodfellow had spilled his tea back yonder. So, he got in his car and drove away. Had you been there, you would have known firsthand that his frantic behavior was a sight to see. Galaxy was facing a long-standing fear of being on his own because he was now afraid to stay in the mansion he had known all his life.

Galaxy, at twenty-one years old, looked even younger. His face had molded itself into symmetry, boasting brown eyes set underneath naturally arched brows. At five foot seven, he had a smallish frame with narrow shoulders and a smooth chest. He found himself unattractive, though no one else did.

But none of that mattered to him now as he fled in his car. Perhaps it was the realization that he couldn't be himself, or maybe it was the crescendo reached as his mother slapped him and called him a faggot after she witnessed his intimacy with another man. Galaxy didn't know how to leave fear behind, so he took it with him, along with his luggage, and left the wealthy side of town, a haunting place you will come to know all too well.

This South Carolina town was called Mansaville, named after Mansa Musa, a West African king whom many considered one of the richest people to have ever lived. It was a fitting name for this all-black municipality that stood as a symbol of independence, with its thriving businesses on Emancipation Boulevard. Most of its residents refused to wear clothes bearing the names of Europeans they would never meet. Instead, the men bought their attire from the local haberdashery that had been owned by Clarence Meriweather, an elderly man whose sartorial masterpieces would have impressed Mansa Musa himself. Women, many adept at sewing, made and sold their pieces to those who were not well versed in creating fashion.

At 33.9 square miles, Mansaville had trees lining every street and forests near every bridge, including the one suspended above the haunted river that was the size of a creek (or a brook, even) but whose history and import had upgraded it to major waterway status as soon as three black kids were thought to have drowned there, only to have their bodies found washed up, each with a knife in their back.

The town had a few lakes too—not haunted, of course, so nighttime skinny-dipping was favored among teens who were exploring their sexuality and twentysomethings whose exploration had been completed while their conquests had not. But no one fished in any body of water. This was a show of respect for the handful of fishermen who did it for a living and kept the market full of fresh fish, all cut on their sides and splayed on ice.

Mansaville and its neighboring towns behaved like trees in a forest, having been next to one another for decades with no proper introduction. The other incorporated areas may have shared the four distinct seasons the Piedmont region had to offer (cold winters, windy springs, humid summers, and cool autumns), but the culture of Mansaville was all its own. When looking at a map, you may fancy it to resemble a tiger facing the Atlantic, with one paw scratching at the next town. Its mouth would appear open as if it were drinking the blood-laced water from the Confederate River, the sinister one that gets its fuel from the same ocean the Europeans crossed to make the blood in the river possible. Native American blood had given way to black blood to create white wealth; and, in Mother Nature's twisted acknowledgment of the past, the river flowed through the tiger in the same direction racism had run through the United States: from east to west.

Situated at what would be the beating heart of the tiger, the crown jewel of this town was Emancipation Bank, launched by Satchel Goodfellow in the 1930s. Born in 1883, just a chronological stone's throw away from slavery, Satchel had also founded and named Mansaville. Although he had branched out to own funeral homes and even a casino and a theater, the bank—the largest of its kind—was the foundation of the Goodfellow dynasty. By the 1970s, their money had grown so much that they were the wealthiest family in South Carolina.

Though gold seemed to rain down on it, there was another side of Mansaville consisting of factory laborers and other working-class residents. The haunted river divided the districts, so the town was connected by two bridges (one for cars, the other an overpass made of rope and a wooden walkway that swayed as you moved across it). Some were courageous enough to cross the river during the day, but none did so at night. It was rumored to have been a place where Confederates had been killed by slaves who refused to remain in subjugation. Howls of dead Confederates could be heard from miles away on some days. On others, their faces were visible in the water, with skeletons looking over their shoulders. Not just a few—an entire army of them on horses, ready at any moment to wreak havoc on Mansaville.

The townspeople had become accustomed to supernatural occurrences and, in most cases, could pretend they weren't happening. Flickering lights, blood falling from the sky, and even sightings of the devil were just parts of their everyday lives. At least once a month, the river would have a red haze above it that would cast a fog over the town. The work of Old Scratch, no doubt, who could be seen wearing a dark cloak while standing on his raft, slowly paddling with a long wooden stick that he had broken from the oak tree—yes, *that* tree.

Mister Tree, the one that stood behind Liberty Baptist Church. On foggy days, all events would be canceled and businesses would be closed because it rained blood, and the river itself would turn into a soupy mixture of blood and screaming skulls. It would boil with froths and foam that burst to let out steam, stifling Mansaville with the smell of death.

In antebellum times, the Confederate skeletons would torture and kill slaves by day and return to their meeting place for supper. The skeletons, whose flesh had since deteriorated, would sit around the table laughing and swapping stories about the black slaves they massacred, the children they stole from crying mothers, and the whips they cracked, leaving scars resembling tree branches on the dark backs of Negroes. The Confederates vehemently believed that compartmentalization of sin was for the weak, as was justification. They had shunned the abolitionists and had emoted particular disdain for free blacks. Confederates became angrier and more violent when laws made it more difficult for them to act on their instincts.

When Mansaville—a financial mecca on one side, a spiritual haven on the other—grew into the town of hope, the skeletons (at the behest of Old Scratch) continued to reside there in the bloody river. The skeletons aimed to destroy the town that forced cognitive dissonance into their empty skulls because it was devastating for them to feel superior while seeing black people exit Emancipation Bank with riches. To slow the rot eating away at the flesh that clung to their bones, they only allowed other Confederate skeletons to join them at the table because, in a room full of serial killers, no one felt like a murderer.

But now it was 1997, and late March had ushered in a South Carolina spring you could, depending on your nature, consider either cool or warm. Galaxy, thinking the former, donned a jacket and a maroon-and-white rugby shirt with an "M" logo representing Morehouse College, a prestigious institution to which his family had decades of ties. Although Galaxy was taking the semester off to deal with the recent death of his father, he thought nothing of his family's legacy as he steered his 1965 Mustang convertible out of his neighborhood, all the while looking at his house in the rearview mirror.

After driving down the road for three miles, he stopped at a filling station. Lucky's Mart had been there since before he was born, and Lenny Simon, the owner, had run the store for nearly half a century. The elderly Mr. Simon and this gas station would be two of the few things Galaxy would miss about this side of Mansaville.

"Howdy, young man."

"Hey, Mr. Simon."

"Ain't seen you in here this early on a Saturday." The snowy-haired man stood there in a green-and-blue flannel shirt and a pair of pleated khakis. Galaxy saw lesions on Mr. Simon's face and neck. The marks hadn't been there during their last encounter. Mr. Simon's skin had a sheen, giving it the appearance of wax that would melt away if it were just ten degrees hotter.

"Well, I decided to get out and get some fresh air." Galaxy placed fifteen dollars on the counter.

"Thank you."

He regarded Galaxy's glossy red eyes, a familiar sight.

"Tell you what, son. Why don't you pull that high-priced car around from the pump and come on in here and have some breakfast?"

"Sir, I . . ."

"It's on the house," Mr. Simon interrupted, holding up the hand adorned with the wedding band that reminded him of his deceased wife. "I'll put some food on the table when you get back in here."

"Okay, sir."

"Sausage biscuit and OJ all right with you?" Mr. Simon asked.

"Yes, sir."

"It's a done deal then, kiddo." Mr. Simon smiled, revealing rotten teeth that were pristine just days ago.

When Galaxy returned, he took off his jacket and sat down at one of the three wooden tables. He took in the scent of the greasy sausage.

Usually, the filling station smelled like an odd combination of ciga-rette smoke and the inviting aroma of food cooking in the back room. Now, however, it was much darker, and the smoke could be seen, not just smelled. The fumes danced around in a haze, cloaking the room in dreariness despite all the windows, which would normally let in natural light. The windows themselves had darkened, making enemies with any sunlight attempting to enter. The glass panes appeared to sweat with dew, except it wasn't clear water. It was a deep burgundy that resembled blood.

Something's not right, Galaxy thought as he felt a tingle in his stomach. He didn't question it further since, like for many residents of Mansaville, the mystical seemed the norm.

As Galaxy examined the substance on the windows, the light bulbs hanging from the ceilings cracked—all three of them at once—assist-ing the smoke and the bloody windows in their quest to bring darkness to the room. On chains that swayed, light bulbs splintered, throwing shards of glass to the floor.

Mr. Simon limped out of the back room holding two plates of pip-ing-hot food. He set one of them in front of Galaxy before placing the other plate on the opposite side of the table. Mr. Simon ambled to the back room again and came back with two glasses of orange juice. Galaxy eyed Mr. Simon's labored gait but didn't inquire about it, nor did he ask about the fog swirling from the drinks.

"The damn lights went out again," the old man said with a grin as he pulled out a lighter and lit two candles, casting a shadow of a skull that went unnoticed because it was on the wall behind Galaxy. Mr. Simon let out a laugh that sounded like a cough. The breath from his cackle killed the flames in one of the candles, forcing the skeleton on the wall to die a second time.

"So, what's on your mind? Something you want to talk about?" asked Mr. Simon.

"No, sir. Not really."

"Talking ain't never hurt nobody." Mr. Simon leaned forward

while reaching for the glass of juice.

"Well . . . ." Tears formed in Galaxy's eyes. He blinked before wiping them.

"Go 'head. Take your time."

Galaxy put his hand to the side of his face and said, "I have to get away from here. I can't take it anymore, Mr. Simon."

"Your mom again?"

"Who else could it be?"

"Yeah, mommas can be real difficult. So, what happened this time?"

"She found out. She caught me in the act and went crazy." He peered into Mr. Simon's eyes.

"She found you with that Barkley fellow?"

Although Barkley had not been involved, Galaxy said, "Yes, sir. How could I have been so stupid?" He broke eye contact, looked at the table, and traced the lines in the wood with an index finger.

"You done heard me say this a million times, but I'll say it again. We all make mistakes. You, me, your mom, Barkley—all of us. You can't beat yourself up about it. You just gotta learn from them and hope tomorrow'll be better than today."

"Can't be any worse," Galaxy said as he took a bite from his biscuit and chased it down with orange juice.

Mr. Simon followed Galaxy's lead by eating his own biscuit before taking a gulp of his drink. The wax-faced older man looked out at the grass across the road as it was being caressed by the wind. Galaxy gazed out at his convertible and wondered how far he could make it on a tank of low-grade gasoline.

After taking the last sip from his glass, the old man glanced across the table at Galaxy, whose left eye had let a tear flow. It traveled the contours of his face, dripping from his chin like a drop of water from an icicle.

"Your mom loves you. She just doesn't know how to deal with your lifestyle. Hell, *most* people can't deal with it." Mr. Simon looked down and continued, "Two days before Pearl died, we got into this big argument over nothing. It seems so foolish now. Had something to do with me not pulling up the weeds in the garden or something like that."

He leaned back and stared at the idle ceiling fan. "I was tired and irritated from being cooped up in here all day, and I was in one of those 'nobody better fuck with me' moods, and she did. She was always a feisty son of a gun. As soon as I came through the front door, she asked me about those damn weeds. Boy, I hated going out in that garden, but Pearl loved it. 'Specially in the spring.

"Anyways, I just snapped and cussed her up one side and down the other. And she matched me word for word." He threw his head back and let out a raspy chuckle. Galaxy joined in, not laughing at what he said but at the way Mr. Simon's hoot resembled a drowning man's gasp for air.

"One thing led to another, and 'fore I knew it, I got in my car and left." He studied Galaxy's face. "You know, sometimes I let my temper get the best of me. I slept in here those two nights in a room back yonder." He pointed at a red door, and Galaxy's eyes followed the direction.

"She was dead two days later. I knew stress could bring on heart failure but—"

"It wasn't your fault," Galaxy interrupted. He had heard around town that Mr. Simon blamed himself for his wife's death.

"Well, I've come to realize that. Took a helluva long time, but I know now. I never let another weed grow in the backyard since she died. I done spent God knows how much money on weed whackers and spray. Hell, I should've been dead considering all those damn chemicals I done breathed in." Laughing at his own wit, he leaned forward in his chair. "The point of my story is . . . running away angry ain't never a good thing 'cause you never know what'll happen while you're gone. I know you think your situation is something different, but trust me, it ain't."

Galaxy nodded his head, though he disagreed.

"I won't pretend like I know what you're going through. I'm just telling you to appreciate what you got 'cause you might not always have it." He looked down at his empty glass. "Now, go on across that bridge to be with the one you love. Don't be afraid of the skeletons. Just hit the gas and cross it so fast even the devil himself can't catch you."

Old Scratch, invisible to both of them, smiled as he held a bloody knife in his hand.

A car pulled up at a gas pump. A middle-aged man got out.

"Well, looks like I got a customer. Things might be starting to pick up. Remember to chase Barkley. He's the one you love," Mr. Simon said.

"Yes, sir."

"You can always talk to me about anything. Don't be a stranger."

"I won't." Galaxy got up and left, not realizing he had just eaten breakfast with the body of a man who had been murdered the previous night.

3

As Galaxy drove down the two-lane country road, he thought of Mr. Simon's appearance. A voice told him something had been amiss, but he tried to ignore the whispers in his own head, welcoming the distraction of the sound of changing gears as his feet pressed on the clutch and the gas pedal. There was no stop sign or red light, but he brought his Mustang to a halt just in front of the bridge. It only spanned about thirty yards, but lore gave it grandeur, making it seem to stretch for miles. He looked to his right and glimpsed the waters where the Confederate skeletons lay submerged in the filth of factory runoff.

A mist rose up from the river, just like it had from the glass of orange juice back at the gas station. Galaxy took a deep breath. Then, with all of the courage he could summon, he took his right foot off of the brake, causing the vehicle to roll back slightly, eased his left foot off of the clutch while pressing the gas pedal, and journeyed across the Confederate River. Galaxy overlooked how the body of water boiled as he crossed the dilapidated bridge. He also failed to notice Old Scratch paddling toward him on a rickety raft, tossing human remains in the car's path. The crackling sounds weren't gravel; they were the depressing music of bones belonging to the corpse of Galaxy's father. Old Scratch wasn't without a sense of humor.

Galaxy found himself in Leroy Walker's community. The roads bore potholes around which he had to maneuver, oftentimes unsuccessfully. When he arrived at what resembled civilization, he saw a set of stoplights (though only one worked) and a playground full of children in unkempt clothing, some playing kickball, others playing freeze tag. To his left, a corner store with two men out front. They drank from bottles in paper bags that were a lighter shade of brown than their hands. They stared at Galaxy as he pulled up.

"He too young to be somebody important."

"Must be passing through."

"Guess the nigga need directions."

Galaxy got out of his car, glanced around, and approached the entrance of the corner store. The two men watched him with the eyes of a hawk—not out of contempt but out of the same fascination Galaxy had with this new environment. Once he was inside the store, the heat from the radiator startled him while he peered at the groceries.

"Hey there," said the cashier, a dark-skinned man with gray hair.

"Hi," Galaxy replied, avoiding eye contact.

"Can I help you with something?"

"I'm just looking around for a sugary snack. I have a sweet tooth today."

"Had one every day when I was your age. Why you think I got these dentures?" the cashier asked with a laugh.

Galaxy smiled and wended his way toward the candy aisle. He was met by an older woman carrying a bag of taffy. Her name was Mary Anne Whitaker. She was dressed in a powder-blue suit and dark pumps. Though it wasn't terribly cold outside, she had on black kidskin gloves, which matched a fur stole that draped around her neck like a serpent. The look she gave him was a mean one. It was as though, with her made-up eyes and wire-framed spectacles, she had reintroduced him to his own triflingness.

When seeing unfamiliar faces, her mission was to force them into believing she wasn't like the poor people over here. Mary Anne wanted them to know she was special, a Granny Smith apple on a McIntosh tree. The scowl on her face had been just as sour and bitter as her chosen fruit. Take your pick of the many menacing expressions that helped Mary Anne chop down sprouting newcomers like Galaxy. Axe wielded, she plopped exact change on the counter and trotted out of the store.

Although Galaxy didn't know her from a bowl of grits, he realized she had status. He would later be made aware that she was the first lady of Liberty Baptist Church and the kind of woman you could trust with your credit card but not with your life. Though his family had enough money to buy the entire town, the way Mary Anne had stared at him lowered his self-worth.

Wishing he were better dressed, Galaxy looked down at his distressed jeans and old shoes. He then retrieved a candy bar from the bottom shelf. He felt awkward asking the merchant for a bag to carry a small item, but he wanted the two men outside to think he had bought a lot more. Exiting the store, he nodded at them. Then he watched Mary Anne as wind crashed into her pastel hat. Without flinching, she hopped into a blue sedan and zoomed away.

Galaxy hurried to his car and sped off, following her, but not in pursuit. He became curious about the factory side of town that seemed stuck in time. Galaxy drove down the street and took a right, just like Mrs. Whitaker, and admired the area's character. Poorly paved streets, rundown houses, and decrepit buildings somehow enhanced its allure.

Not caring that he had lost sight of the blue sedan, Galaxy continued to drive down the quiet, tree-lined street, using the directions his ex-boyfriend Barkley had given him to get to the park. He drove farther and detected no traces of major development until, to his left, he spotted a wooden sign with green words that had faded since it was painted some decades prior by a soon-to-be ordained Johnny Whitaker and his best friend. Weathered but bold, it read, "Liberty Baptist Church" in crooked letters. The sign's flaws gave it authenticity, proving it belonged in this imperfectly perfect section of Mansaville. Galaxy set eyes on the charming little church, perched atop a hill at the end of a curvy road. The dim white of the building gave it the appearance of being in the distance, though it was just yards away. Its steeple was a short one with a small cross on top that almost blended in with the green of the trees beside it, but it was noticeable nonetheless, as were the double doors at the top of a set of concrete stairs. It was much too modest to look like a church that attempted to reach the heavens, but to Galaxy, it was an amazing structure.

He loved the building despite what it represented. Having rejected church as an institution, Galaxy's sentiments surprised even himself. He had heard stories about Liberty Baptist, so seeing it had made his journey worthwhile. Not thinking that stumbling upon the place of worship would be part of his day, Galaxy had expected it to be a massively elegant piece of architecture, but it wasn't. That was owed to its lack of pretension (the chipped paint, the rough road leading to it, the wild vines that climbed up the edifice and folded over the charcoal-gray shingles on the roof). A landmark and beacon of hope, Liberty Baptist stood as the centerpiece of Mansaville's factory side.

Galaxy drove past a strip of houses and voyaged until arriving at his destination to meet Barkley, the guy who had taken his virginity. He parked near a basketball court full of men playing a pickup game. Not wanting to draw attention, Galaxy was relieved that the contest captivated everyone. No one noticed him—except for Barkley Jenkins Jr., the twenty-six-year-old man standing on the side of the court. Barkley was tall, muscular, and thick in all the right places. Though his face was merely handsome, his body had the appeal of well-executed graffiti—beautiful yet criminal. If he had been naked on the auction block in antebellum times, his looks would have been called expensive, but now, he was just a fine-ass nigga.

Galaxy could feel his asshole getting moist while looking at Barkley. Maybe it was because of the black shorts that clung to Barkley's legs—or perhaps it was that damn walk. Judging from the bulge in those shorts, you could tell his dick was the front porch to a house of pleasure. Having sat on that porch many a trashy night, Galaxy watched in lust as his ex stepped toward the car and tapped on the passenger window. Galaxy rolled it down slightly.

"You don't have to be scared. I know this ain't your side of town," Barkley said, exposing his top row of teeth.

His teeth weren't perfect, but his smile certainly was. Barkley's grin prompted Galaxy to roll the window all the way down, letting in a chilly waft of air.

"You called me saying you needed my help. Said you wanted to crash at my place," Barkley said.

"I do."

"I got you, little man, but we gotta keep it on the hush-hush for now."

"I understand. You're embarrassed of me," Galaxy muttered while holding his head down and blinking.

"I'm not embarrassed, little man. I just ain't ready to put it out there yet. You feel me?"

"Okay," Galaxy responded.

Barkley leaned into the window. "Did you miss me?"

Galaxy smiled and said, "Yes, I did."

"Look at you. You're cheesing like a motherfucker."

"Whatever," Galaxy responded.

Barkley looked at the back seat and asked, "Where's your shit?"

"It's in the trunk."

"How much you pack?"

"A week's worth," Galaxy said.

"You'll be with me more than a week." Barkley smiled and leaned farther into the car. With the relaxed voice of a cigar smoker getting head, he added, "Once you get this dick again, you'll want to stay with me for life."

"What-the-fuck-ever," Galaxy replied, his ears becoming ashtrays to catch every ember.

Barkley laughed and said, "I got to holler at my boys real quick. I'll be right back."

He returned and got in the passenger side. Galaxy beamed and reached out to grab his hand. The hand-holding was accompanied with eye contact that assured them. Barkley saw an old friend in Galaxy's eyes and found comfort in his soft, delicate hand. They wanted to speak again. Galaxy fixed his mouth to say something, but no words came out. So enthralled with Galaxy, Barkley also wanted to converse since he had questions about what had forced his former boyfriend to leave home. The inquiry would have to wait. Right now, he focused on Galaxy's face, a countenance he hadn't seen in two years.

Barkley wanted to heap praise on Galaxy but instead offered, "I still love you, little man."

"I love you, too, sugar."

Being called that reminded Barkley of his grandmother. He and Galaxy felt whole in that moment, as if they were sitting on the front pew listening to the most comforting gospel number, a song you have never heard but somehow know its lyrics.

You may have seen people in church sway when the spirit moved them. Well, it touched Galaxy in this moment, so he too just rocked back and forth. Lord knows, that was all he could do.

PART II
Trade

4

I miss my sweet Barkley. He was my only grandchild, and boy was he something else. Used to get in a bunch of mess every day, but I couldn't bring myself to whip him. But his daddy, Barkley Sr. . . . Lord, have mercy! He would get at little Barkley with a switch every chance he got. He'd make Barkley go pull the switch from the bushes himself. By the time Junior was three, the bushes next to the porch ain't have no twigs. Wasn't nothing but little stubs and roots. They looked bad, but knowing how they got that way tickled me to death.

Barkley Sr. didn't understand Junior. You got to let kids be kids. Let them get in a little trouble sometimes. Junior would get into some from the time he was a toddler all the way up until the Lord took me up yonder. I knowed why Junior was acting up and cutting a fool the way he did. That come from inside. I knowed he was different because he used to fight all the time. He wasn't even fighting about nothing. Always had his chest out like he was trying to be the man of the house before he even went to junior high. Senior wouldn't allow it. They used to argue, but I told Junior not to talk back to his daddy. The Lord never put up with lip.

He couldn't stand his father, and it tore me up. I'm just glad his daddy didn't know the truth. He would've killed Junior and his friend Paul too. I caught them once. They was kissing out behind the church, right in front of Mister Tree. I was scared they was gonna wake that tree up, but they didn't. Thank God for that. And thank God they had the good sense to hide they secret 'cause them church folks back then wouldn't allow it. It didn't matter to me. Junior and Paul was just as good as anybody. They hearts beat just like everybody else's. I can say that now, but back then . . . help me, Jesus. They would've thrown me out the church—maybe out the whole town—just for loving my grandson the way Jehovah made him.

He loved me too, and I spoiled him with my cooking. He took a liking to my cream corn and them good ol' biscuits I used to whip up. Long before he was even old enough to eat grown folks' food, his little hands could sop up some molasses with a biscuit. Don't get me started on my sweet potato pie. He would show out if someone ate the last piece. I would hide it just to mess with him.

I miss that child, but I know he'll be up here with me one day . . . in this mansion up high.

5

Once again, Grandma Sarah was right. Barkley Jenkins Jr. hated his father. He despised the way his dad gave him beatings. After reaching his twenties, Barkley's newfound strength married rebellion. The nuptials brought on retaliation that reverberated throughout the factory side of Mansaville.

Barkley didn't decide to leave the dilapidated two-bedroom home he had known all his life. Instead, an eviction notice disguised as an arrest warrant forced him to find government housing with more floor space and a larger kitchen but a lot less freedom. It seemed as though he was arraigned, tried, and convicted before his dad's funeral.

As he rode away from the courthouse in shackles, to his left stood Liberty Baptist Church, where a year earlier Reverend Johnny Whitaker had preached about the Ten Commandments. Though the minister believed all of them to be important, he seemed to emphasize two: "Honor thy father and thy mother" and "Thou shalt not kill." Sarah Jenkins, in her husky voice, used to always tell her grandson, "You disrespect your parents, and it'll shorten your days." Young Barkley never listened to her, nor did he take advice from Reverend Whitaker.

As the good old reverend preached from Exodus that Sabbath day, Barkley had skipped church to play cards with Tyrone, Paul, and another male friend who would later die of cancer. The adults always gave the kids pocket change so they could have money to tithe. Instead of giving it to the church, the children used it to gamble while playing spades. That Sunday, Barkley and his playing partner won a five-dollar bill, five case quarters, four dimes, and a penny. Once again, Barkley Jenkins Jr. was on top.

But presently, after two years of legal squabbling, the state released Barkley the previous month, just after Valentine's Day. His sole regret about being incarcerated was that he didn't get to see his beloved grandmother before she died of a disease that had always haunted the Jenkins family. At ten years old, sugar claimed the life of her father. Two decades later, she lost Blacky (her only sibling) to the same illness.

But that was a long time ago.

Now, as Barkley and Galaxy were entering Sarah's old home, the odor of mothballs and the lingering smell of weed made Galaxy take a step back.

"You good?" Barkley asked.

"Yes, I'm good," Galaxy said in a tone that was softer than his already gentle voice.

"I'll put your shit in the room. Sit down and get comfortable," Barkley said.

The last command seemed like a tall order because clear plastic covered the couch on which Galaxy sat. The furniture had been in the same spot for the better part of a decade. A floor-model television rested on the brown carpet. The word "Rutherford" provided the only shine on a TV encased in manufactured wood. On top of the television sat a gold urn containing the ashes of Grandma Sarah. It, too, had been unmoved for years.

"I got the room ready for you. Come on."

"Okay," Galaxy responded. The friction from the couch's plastic covering and Galaxy's denim created a creaking noise, making him sigh. He shuffled toward the main quarters of this two-bedroom house, passing by Sarah's picture hanging crooked next to Leonardo da Vinci's *The Last Supper*, with Jesus sitting in the middle of a table of people, one rumored to have been a woman. Like a woman himself, Galaxy sashayed across the linoleum floors and crossed the threshold of his new bedroom, which had a king-sized bed covering most of the floor space. The gold-and-black combination of sheets brought more disgust to Galaxy's face.

"What's wrong, little man?" Barkley asked while inching closer to Galaxy.

"Nothing. I'm good," Galaxy said, echoing the lie he told upon entering the house.

"Talk to me. Tell me what's wrong." Barkley leaned his head sideways.

"I'm just tired."

"You can take a nap. I got to go back out anyway."

"Go back out and do what?" Galaxy asked.

"Handle some business."

"What business?"

"What do you think, little man?"

"I understand," Galaxy said in an almost-whisper.

"I got to make that paper. How you think I bought all this fancy shit?" Barkley pointed around the room.

Galaxy smiled.

"All right, little man. I'm out."

"Okay. Lock the door."

Barkley laughed. "Nigga, this ain't the hood."

"None of Mansaville is," Galaxy added.

"Come here."

Galaxy moved forward, stood on his toes, and wrapped his arms around Barkley's shoulders and neck.

"You know I got you." Barkley loosened the hug.

"I know."

Barkley kissed him on the forehead and left.

Galaxy took off all of his clothes and went to get his suitcase out of the closet where he rightly assumed Barkley had put it. Delighted to find a set of fresh linens on the top shelf, Galaxy pulled them down. The color scheme of the bedsheets (Tiffany Blue and brown) reminded him of his former home on the industrial side of the river. He held the linens like they were a toddler and placed them on top of his luggage, fearing the floor would be too dirty. He undressed the bed and removed the slips from the four pillows that had been scattered near the black wooden headboard.

Still in the nude, Galaxy made up the bed, strolled toward the doorway, and thought, *I'm home.*

⊙᙭᙭᙭Ϙ

Once Galaxy had settled into the house, he lay on Barkley's bed. The sound of water pouring from the showerhead calmed him. He listened while Barkley bathed. Galaxy turned on the television and watched a male soul singer stand in front of a choir and belt out an inspirational song—a much-needed number since Galaxy's life had changed so much in less than a day. Audience members cheered for the man holding the microphone as he brought the song to a close with a deep note.

The water stopped just as the singer took a bow. As the scene faded into screen credits, a naked Barkley emerged from the bathroom with a slick film covering his body, giving his chocolate skin luster. Between his thick thighs—there his dick was, swinging slowly, swaying from side to side—a grandfather clock's pendulum of manhood. With each dangling motion, a second disappeared. Galaxy watched a minute's worth before Barkley took notice. Both knew what time it was. Dressed in a pair of briefs, Galaxy got out of bed and strutted toward him. There was no genuflecting, for Galaxy was much too greedy to take a knee. So, he took two—right in front of the towering clock.

Then . . . .

Galaxy used his mouth to neither cheer like the audience nor croon like the soul singer; rather, to Barkley's delight, Galaxy used it to stop time.

6

Three days after Galaxy had moved in with Barkley, they found themselves in the kitchen. While Galaxy sat at the wobbly table, Barkley stood in front of the stove, steam rising out of the cast-iron skillet. Shirtless and barefoot, Barkley wore a gold chain and a pair of jeans, the upper locks of his pubic hair visible on the front of his body, the top of his ass crack observable on the other side. Thinking there was something sexy about a man who knew how to cook, Galaxy watched without speaking.

Barkley, also quiet, took the country ham and scrambled eggs out of the skillet and placed them onto two plates, his containing twice as much. He turned down the range and put two pieces of bread into the bubbling grease in the skillet and pressed each slice down with a spatula, flipped them over, and pushed down again. Once the bread browned, he put the slices on the plates.

"All right, little man. It's time to eat," Barkley said while carrying the plates to the table. He retrieved plastic cups from the cabinet, added ice to them, and drowned the cubes in sweet tea he had made using his grandmother's recipe. A touch of lemonade, a splash of orange juice with pulp, cane sugar, and even a little brown sugar to give it a honeyed kick.

"You called me talking about how you needed to move in. I said yes without asking why. So, what's up, little man? What's the deal?" Barkley put the cups on the table and sat down before adding, "I wanted to wait a few days to ask. I could tell you didn't want to talk about it, but now it's time."

"You're right. I didn't want to talk about it. I don't want to talk about it now, either," Galaxy said.

"You owe me an explanation, little man. I need to know why you—"

"I got caught."

"Caught doing what?"

"My momma got home early and walked in on me having sex with another dude," Galaxy said.

"Oh, so you let another nigga fuck you, and you want my help? You got some nerve, little man." Barkley squared his shoulders.

"I don't have to explain myself to you. We're not together."

"I know we ain't together, but you're asking for my help. So, you need to explain," Barkley said.

"That's fair." Galaxy put his head down.

"I know it's fair, little nigga. Start talking." Barkley raised his voice but relaxed his shoulders.

Galaxy took a breath. "Okay. Here's what happened. I was walking home from the coffee shop down the street, and a white dude approached me."

"A white dude in Mansaville? You should've known it wouldn't end right."

"Let me finish," Galaxy said with a slight frown.

"All right, but watch your tone when you're talking to Big Daddy."

Galaxy laughed. "Anyway, he was walking toward me. And when he got close, he smiled. That's what drew me in. His teeth were flawless. His eyes were beautiful, too. Bright green. He said, 'Hi.' His head was tilted to the side when he said it, and that did it for me. I know he saw me looking at the bulge in his shorts because he grabbed his dick and rubbed on it to make it bigger. That's when I knew what was up.

"He said, 'I see you looking at it. Don't be afraid of the urge,' and flashed a smile.

"Next thing I knew, we were in my bedroom, and he was hitting it doggy style. I knew something was off because his hands felt cold on my waist. But the dick was so good I ignored it." Galaxy sighed.

"You good, little man?" Barkley scooched forward.

Fire had come out of Galaxy's back during the encounter he was describing, but he wasn't ready to reveal this to Barkley.

Galaxy continued, "He pulled out, flipped me over, put my legs over his shoulders, and stuck it back in. I could see his face in that position. His eyes did this crazy thing. They went from green to red. His pupils and the whites of his eyes turned black. Blood started forming in them and dripped on my face. I couldn't stop him. It's like I was paralyzed. He just kept going. He was laughing like a madman. When I tried to yell, a big snake came out of nowhere and wrapped around my mouth.

"That's when my momma walked in and screamed. The guy's eyes had turned back to green, and the snake disappeared right before she got there. She turned away and left. I was terrified. He got off me and put on his clothes without touching them. They just floated from the floor and attached to him. Then he looked at me and smiled."

"And?" Barkley asked.

"And he just left," Galaxy replied.

Barkley shook his head and said, "Damn, nigga. You had sex with the devil."

7

Later that day, Barkley left to get lunch. Taking advantage of the alone time, Galaxy retrieved a pair of Barkley's dirty boxer briefs from the hamper. After sniffing the crotch area while closing his eyes, he put the underwear on. Although the garment was too big for him, he loved that its cotton fabric was still damp from sweat. The sound of Barkley's car pulling into the driveway prompted Galaxy to take off the underwear and resume wearing his own clothes: a pair of shorts, flip-flops, and a T-shirt.

"I got us lunch," Barkley said as he entered the house. "Come to the kitchen."

"Okay," Galaxy yelled from the bedroom as he made his way to the table where Barkley was taking a seat. In front of them were sub sandwiches, bags of barbecue chips, and two bottles of Coke.

"Eat up, little man." Barkley pointed at the food.

Galaxy sat in the chair opposite him.

"Are you comfortable here yet?"

"I think so." Galaxy shrugged his shoulders.

"This is your home now. I told you that."

"It's still very new," Galaxy responded.

"I get it, little man."

They ate in silence until Barkley asked, "Is there anything about you I should know? Any secrets?"

"Well, I've never told anybody this, but when I'm doing chores around the house, I have to be naked."

Barkley smiled. "What kind of chores?"

"Any kind of cleaning, especially vacuuming. For some reason, I have to take off my clothes and vacuum naked."

"That's sexy as fuck." Barkley smiled again, but more broadly.

"Shut up. I'm trying to be serious." Galaxy opened a bag of chips. "I don't understand it. It's just what I do."

"I'm good with that."

"Of course, you are." Galaxy retrieved a chip from the bag. "Even when I make up the bed, I have to be naked. I'll take off the clothes I slept in, tidy the bed, and put my clothes right back on."

Barkley laughed.

"It's not funny," Galaxy said, though he himself was beaming. "What about you? What weird shit you got going on?"

"Mine is a little more serious," Barkley said. "It's kind of a whole nother thing, but I need to let you know." He exhaled and rubbed his forehead.

"What is it?" Galaxy put down the bag of chips.

"Something I did in the joint."

"Okay. What?" Galaxy asked.

"I raped somebody."

Galaxy's eyes opened wide. "You raped somebody? Who?"

"He was a white dude. About five eleven, kinda muscular, but kinda not. He stepped to me at the outdoor gym. Security didn't fuck with us when we worked out. They let us do whatever."

"So, what happened?" Galaxy asked.

"He had been talking shit to me for months, but I always let it go. This time, I talked shit back. He was one of them neo-Nazis. He swung at me, and I moved out the way. I swung back and knocked him down. I could tell he was dizzy, but he was still conscious. So, I stomped on his stomach one good time to knock the wind out of him, turned him over, pulled his pants down, and spit in his ass to get it wet. Then I pulled my pants down, got on top of him, and raped him. The other dudes just stood there and watched. I pounded him out real good too, little man. That cracker never fucked with me after that."

"Security didn't see *any* of it?" Galaxy asked as his dick was getting hard.

"They saw it. The three guards on duty were black, so they didn't care about a Nazi getting raped. They just looked the other way."

"Wow." Galaxy put a hand to his chest. "Do you feel bad about doing it?"

"No, I don't. He swung at me first, so I raped him in self-defense."

With a dick that was now rock hard, Galaxy realized Barkley was the kind of nigga every sissy wanted . . . a piece of trade. Any guy who was man enough to rape another man was strong and sexy. For this, he fell in love with Barkley.

Galaxy would have been even more in love if he had been there to witness Barkley's prowess in person. Barkley had showed no mercy when raping the Caucasian inmate. He hollowed out that white boy's ass like a jack-o'-lantern, and the only seed he left in it was cum.

PART III

The Immaculate
Deception

8

Mary Anne never had good sense. The poor girl didn't know how to act to save her life. I was the only one to witness how she got that scar 'cross her right eye. It was on a Sunday, right after church. The grown folks used to stay inside to talk. Some used to go out front with the chillun and watch them play. When we was kids, the girls would play hopscotch in front of ol' Liberty while the boys raced each other up and down the road. It happened when we was about nine years old. I even 'member the little dresses we had on. I had on a light-green dress with flowers on it. Had plaits in my hair with little plastic bows at the ends. Mary Anne wore light purple. Her momma had hot-combed her hair straight enough to put it in a ponytail. They tied it up in a beautiful purple scarf. She came up to me and asked me to go out behind the church where the big open field was. Wasn't nothing in that field except a tree: Mister Tree. It was a great big oak. It had branches that fanned out twenty feet. Everyone knowed it was the hanging spot a long time ago. Black folks had been hung on that tree back when whites lived there and strung 'em up. The white folks done gone, but the tree stayed right there. It was an ugly thang, too. Evil looking— had sticky moss growing up the sides, the bark almost looked gray and ashed over. It would sing out in the middle of the night sometimes. A song about some skeleton army coming to kill everybody. It had a deep voice that echoed in the wind when it sang about dead bodies riding horses into the town.

No one cut that tree down 'cause they didn't know what would happen if they did. But Mary Anne was always the one to test the waters, and I was dumb enough to go down there with her. I 'clare that girl could get me to do the craziest things. I followed her down the hill to the part where the ground got flat and the field opened up. The tree was right there. Wasn't sangin' about nothing, though. It was just standing tall.

Mary Anne said, "I don't like that tree." She was hoping it could hear her.

I said, "I don't, either." I had the good sense to whisper.

"You know how to get rid of something you don't like?" Mary Anne asked.

Then I asked, "How?"

She spoke words I'll never forget. She said, "All you have to do is close your eyes, and it'll disappear. If I close my eyes and run toward the tree, I'll be okay because the tree won't be there no more."

So, she closed her eyes, held up her dress at the sides, and ran toward the tree as fast as she could. I don't know what she was thinking. She ran right into Mister Tree and it made a sound that scared everybody. The tree howled. It was a hollow-sounding howl that echoed into a song. "Them skeletons gonna ride they horses. They gonna get they swords and kill everybody." *It wasn't just one voice this time. It was a whole choir singing right loud. Mary Anne's face hit the tree as hard as anything I had ever witnessed. She was on the ground with blood going down her face and a gash that went from her right eye down to her cheek. Grown folks heard Mister Tree's song, picked up they Bibles for protection, and ran down the hill to the open field where the tree stood. They surrounded Mary Anne and shook they heads.*

"That girl never listens," her momma said. By then she was tending to Mary Anne and asking someone to get some help. Mary Anne was screaming and everybody else was whispering to the Lord. Mister Tree was steady watching everybody, and he got so quiet. After he stopped sangin', Mister Tree didn't say a word. He never did.

9

Just after getting married, Mary Anne and her husband, Reverend Johnny Whitaker, took a walk. They made their way past Liberty Baptist to the end of Church Street, which was just a dirt road. The weather afforded the town heat that forced the Whitakers out of most of their clothes. Johnny was in a beat-up pair of khaki shorts with no shirt. His leather shoes dangled, as he held them by the laces. At six foot two, possessing a slim but toned build and an Afro, Johnny towered over his wife. Like his expensive shoes, his skin was dark and smooth. Mary Anne's African American skin, however, was as light as her beige sundress. This garment was damp from sweat, so it had been pulled completely off, leaving her in just a shiny slip. She clutched her shoes and her dress as she followed her husband.

"Where are we going, Johnny? You know we ain't supposed to be in these woods. It's where the skeletons are."

"Mary Anne, you can't believe all that foolishness. That's just some stuff old folks made up to keep us from leaving the factory."

"I don't know about this, Johnny." Mary Anne grabbed his left hand.

"Trust me, baby." He tightened his grip on her hand while guiding her through the woods.

"It's getting dark. We wusta get back home," Mary Anne said.

"Baby, you got to live some. You know I can protect you."

The sun had begun to tuck itself under the horizon, giving the crescent moon center stage. Too nervous to perform just yet, the moon hid behind gray clouds.

"There it is, Mary Anne."

"Lord, it sho' is. It's that haunted river."

He waived his hand as if to shoo her away and said, "Girl, it ain't bitmo haunted. Ain't no ghosts."

"Skeletons." Mary Anne raised her voice.

"Ain't no skeletons, either," Johnny said.

"Yes, there is."

"Stop talking, and get to the river," Johnny said.

"You can go, but I'm staying right here." With one hand, she held her dress. The other was in a fist against her hip.

"Okay. Wait here." Johnny plodded down the hill.

"Lord, protect him."

"See? It ain't haunted." Johnny knelt, cupped water in his hands, and drank it. He ignored the faint taste of blood because the coolness was so refreshing.

"Nigga, you crazy," Mary Anne said.

As Johnny swallowed, a chill came over his body. He shivered and danced, flailing his arms and kicking his legs up. Johnny wanted to stop, but a force controlled him.

He made his way up the hill and danced in front of Mary Anne, who laughed so hard she missed the water bubbling in the Confederate River.

He stopped.

"Take that slip off, girl."

"Here?"

"Just do it." Johnny's voice was airy as he pulled his shorts down around his ankles and stepped out of them, standing there naked.

"Lord, have mercy. Put your clothes back on."

He bent down, grabbed the bottom of her slip, and slowly stood up while pulling it over her head, removing the article of clothing, so that she, too, was completely exposed.

"Somebody gonna see us," Mary Anne said with a smile.

"Lay down, girl."

She did.

Johnny got on his knees and spread her legs before getting on top of her. He kissed her. She could taste the blood from the river water on his tongue, but the passion made her dismiss it. Powerfully aroused, he penetrated her vagina and stroked. Mary Anne moaned while looking up at the moon. So overcome with desire, neither noticed Johnny's penis had turned into a snake. He continued to thrust his pelvis, causing the serpent to move in and out of her. Before the moon could hide behind another cloud, the snake opened its mouth and spit its venom inside her. Johnny trembled in pleasure.

"This feels so good," Mary Anne whispered.

As the venomous snake turned back into a penis, the moon cast its light across Johnny's smiling face. He was unaware that his manhood was once a slithering beast that had just planted an evil seed.

10

In the initial years of their marriage, Mary Anne would wake up early on Sunday morning to prepare breakfast for her husband. But one particular Sunday would alter the course of her life, her husband's life, and the lives of everyone on both sides of the Confederate River. After getting out of bed, she washed her face, put on a light-blue housedress, and went to the kitchen.

While reaching for a loaf of bread, Mary Anne felt something around her neck. She turned to the window behind her, eyed the reflection, and realized it was a snake—a black one with a red stripe running from its head to its tail. Just as she tried to scream, the snake silenced her by coiling its body around her mouth and the back of her head, just above her neck where the hot comb's burn marks were. Mary Anne fell to the floor, her left side hitting the linoleum without making a sound. She rolled over on her back as the snake maintained its firm grasp. While turning her head, Mary Anne spotted a large spider creeping toward her, its dark gray abdomen possessing fur that had a sheen, its legs making faint clanking sounds of metal hitting metal. With the sharp ends of its legs, the spider cut a slit in the middle of her housedress, exposing her belly and private parts. It paralyzed everything but her face.

The spider, with the melody of tolling metal, pulled itself between her legs, using its own dark legs to open her vagina before crawling inside. Mary Anne groaned as the spider made its way through her cervix and into her uterus. Once there, it wrapped its limbs around the baby's head and dragged him out of her. The spider's back legs came out first, then its large abdomen, now covered in blood. The infant opened his eyes once the fresh air hit his face. He giggled as his body writhed in a puddle of Mary Anne's blood. The spider shrank before inching into the baby's mouth. The snake relaxed its grip, mimicked the shrinking of the spider, and slithered into the infant's eye. Still giggling and covered in his mother's blood and placenta, the child stood up and waddled to her.

When she got a good look at him, his Caucasian skin startled her. Even in shock, Mary Anne had the presence of mind to realize she had just given birth to Old Scratch, the devil himself. His skin tone was striking, as were his green eyes—the most beautiful Mary Anne had ever seen, for they shone like emeralds, sparkling with hate.

"Hi, Mom," Baby Scratch said before smiling, exposing a mouth full of teeth, all in perfect alignment.

Mary Anne gasped, with her fear of the serpent's return suppressing her urge to scream. Baby Scratch saw a knife that had fallen to the floor and ambled toward it, snickering as he picked it up, an effort that required both of his small, weak hands. He then left the room and the house to go to the Confederate River to be raised by the skeletons. All the while, Mary Anne cried, thinking she might never get to nurse her oldborn baby.

11

They all sat in the pews, listening to the choir at Liberty Baptist Church. Some were praise dancing, stomping to the beat of the music. The men seemed to lift their knees up higher than the women, who were holding their dresses at the sides while they too stomped to the sound of tambourines and handclaps. Others quivered while catching the Holy Ghost.

"How I got over," the soprano sang as the people in the church repeated her words in unison.

"Take your time," an old man shouted.

"Make it plain," another yelled out.

"All right now."

"Yes, sir."

"Hallelujah."

The soprano sang in a way that bordered on a holler and a cry for help.

At least a dozen congregants waved their hands in praise. Others rocked back and forth.

The music stopped.

So did the dancing and waving of hands.

Reverend Johnny Whitaker, Mary Anne's husband, took to the stage.

"That girl sho' can sing, amen?" he asked.

"Amen," some replied.

The reverend continued, "The world is in a nasty place right now. Women walking 'round in provocative clothes. Black men selling drugs. Out-of-wedlock kids. Men sleeping with men. Women sleeping with women." He wiped his forehead with a cloth. "It's ungodly," he said.

He locked eyes with a gentleman sitting in the third pew. This young man was a prostitute the reverend had hired the previous month.

The minister ditched his sermon and said, "I think it's time for another song."

The crowd jumped up and danced again as the music started. The reverend's male prostitute was outdancing them all.

The music intensified as Reverend Whitaker went back to his chair and sat next to his wife.

"I love you, baby," he said.

"I love you too," Mary Anne replied before whispering to herself, "I'm glad I married a man of God."

The reverend grabbed her hand and smiled as he looked down at the diamond ring he had bought her with last week's tithes.

12

Nothing triggered Mary Anne's anxiety like a coincidence. Her overactive mind connected unrelated things. Like the time she strangled her cat to death, believing it could hear her intrusive thoughts telling her she had once had sex with her brother, though she was an only child. Or when she whacked the television with a shovel, believing those on the screen were watching her get undressed. Or the time she picked up a trowel and went outside to plant seeds to grow her own vegetables, believing the old lady who owned the farmers market had tried to poison her. Mary Anne had never properly nourished the garden, so nothing ever grew. When her husband was away, she would go out back to pick imaginary vegetables and pretend to cook them for her baby who had abandoned her with a knife in his hand. Knowing she would never be able to get pregnant again hurt her in ways nothing else could, except when she looked at her dying mother in the hospital and asked, "Who is my real father?" Her mother had refused to answer, so Mary Anne left her to die alone.

She had to be some kind of crazy to have her momma's funeral the same day she had the wedding ceremony to renew her and Johnny's vows. The crazy child even sported her wedding dress to the funeral. She made her husband and the groomsmen wear tuxedos. Leave it to Mary Anne to turn groomsmen into pallbearers.

Two weeks after the wedding/funeral, Mary Anne rummaged through her mother's belongings in search of clues about her own background. In the kitchen, underneath a piece of wax paper, she found her birth certificate, if it could be called that. Because of poor recordkeeping, it was handwritten on the back of the deed to her mother's house, which now belonged to her and Johnny. On the document, in cursive, it revealed her real birth name: Mary Anne Goodfellow.

"Sweet Jesus," she whispered, as memories of her upbringing flooded her mind. Mary Anne shook her head while thinking of the times her family had to eat peanut butter sandwiches for breakfast, lunch, and dinner. Having to piss and shit in an outhouse, or even worse, emptying the slop jar. She recalled helping her mother put a tin tub outside to catch rainwater for them to drink until the man she believed to be her father could cash his check to pay a plumber.

So, at the sight of her birth certificate, Mary Anne did something she hadn't done since that horrible childhood: She wept salty tears. The most brackish teardrop signified her being lied to and told her birth surname was Smith. Everyone in Mansaville knew the Goodfellow name and the wealth that came with it, yet she had grown up poor with a mother who had to leave town every day to, as her mother put it, "clean them white folks' houses."

Although Mary Anne's own house wasn't clean, the devastation of knowing the truth forced her to ignore household tasks. Instead, she curled up in bed to seek rest.

Not an eternal rest.

Rather, a brief one.

Though she would wake up wondering if she was still alive.

PART IV

The Protector

13

I know you been wondering why nobody outside of Mansaville know about all the evil stuff that go on. The blood coming from the sky, them skeletons, and the devil. Well, it's 'cause of fear, the most powerful emotion. Once everybody heard about what happened to Leroy Walker, the whole town started to keep they mouth shut. I did, too, even though I know silence ain't no Negro's friend.

Leroy was out riding his bike one day, and he made it all the way out of Mansaville. He had planned to go on home, but he stopped at a store to get some water. Lord, why did he do that, knowing full well he was in Sugarlake County, where them white folks be? He got to talking to one of them and started telling about how blood rained from the sky every month in Mansaville. He didn't know he was talking to a dead body that belonged to somebody the devil had stabbed. See? Old Scratch kill white folks too.

Leroy didn't know no better, and that liquor got at him. He was known for being a drunk. So, he was steady talking. That dead body didn't like Leroy telling the devil's business. The blood rain wasn't for everybody to know. So, time Leroy left the store, the dead man and three white men beat him to death with pipes. Blood was everywhere.

The devil had them white boys take Leroy's body to Mansaville, and they left a note on it saying Leroy talked too much and he should've kept his mouth shut about that sky blood. From then on, nobody talked to outside folks about the Confederate rain or about the devil either. Back then, the rain had only happened twice, so word didn't get out. Now it never will 'cause the devil done scared everybody into hush.

That's how they get us. They make an example out of one, and the rest just keep quiet.

No one asked how the corner store got named after Leroy. Well, the devil did it, so black folks wouldn't forget Leroy's mouth was what got him killed. White folks get they power that way. They trick you and do stuff to make you keep on hushing.

14

Grandma Sarah told you why black folks kept quiet, but she didn't mention why they stayed. You see, they remained in Mansaville out of a bizarre combination of fear and pride. Sure, the devil seemingly had the ability to draw them back in, like he had done to Galaxy. But it was phantom power. The townspeople could have packed up and left, but Leroy's demise convinced them that leaving would have deadly consequences, so they resided there, generation after generation. The rich ones like the Goodfellows stood their ground out of defiant pride, refusing to let the devil and the mysterious rain scare them away from a town they had built.

But now, the residents of Mansaville weren't thinking of their town's history, nor were they aware that the sky was about to cry tears of blood because, like the wicked corpse and the three white men who gave Leroy Walker no warning, the clouds didn't afford Mansaville's residents any notice that a bad Confederate storm was coming. Galaxy, however, had felt a spirit come over him. Flames came out of his back as he sat in the passenger side of his Mustang, waiting for Barkley to come out of the corner store. The emergence of his fire started as a tingle that intensified as the clouds gathered above the town. This time, the sapphire flames were different, for they took shape. Fire in the form of wings shot out of Galaxy's back as he covered his mouth to hold in a scream. He looked to his right and saw a wing made of his blue fire. On his other side, another of the same size fluttered with identical fervor, hurling sparks throughout the car. The wings hugged him gently. The coolness of the flames relaxed him. The blaze eventually turned into sparks and disappeared, leaving behind a chilly breeze.[*]

"I'm glad no one saw that," Galaxy said to himself.

Barkley came out of Leroy's Corner Store carrying Olde English beer in a small paper bag in one hand and a Black & Mild cigar in the other.

"We have to get back home. The Confederate rain is coming," Galaxy said.

"How do you know, little man?" Barkley asked as he started the car. "I didn't hear Mister Tree howling."

"I just know." With Galaxy's words, they gave ear to a wail resembling that of a dying wolf. A gust of wind shook the vehicle.

"Okay, little man. Let's go," Barkley said.

They sped off and found themselves pulling into their driveway minutes later. On the porch of the house across the street, Mary Anne and her best friend, Betty Mae, were engaging in their usual banter. Despite Mister Tree's cries, both women were unaware that Confederate rain was about to come down. Almost every Saturday for the past ten years, they would sit on the porch and gossip over beverages and baked goods. And this Saturday would be no different. They drank the sweet tea that Mary Anne had mixed with lemons, adding a tangy flavor Betty Mae relished. And they each ate a slice of the pound cake Mary Anne made the previous night to deal with the hollowness of an empty house.

"There goes Barkley," Mary Anne said.

"Uh-hum, I see. Eyes ain't what they used to be, but I see him," Betty Mae responded. "What is he doing driving that Mustang?"

"That car done been in that driveway for a while now. Me and Johnny been trying to figure out whose it was."

"Who is that little boy with him?" Betty Mae asked.

---

[*] The fire didn't burn people or objects that were not a threat. So, things on his person and items around him were not damaged. The fire only burned hot when there was danger. Even then, it would just destroy the menacing threat, sparing all else.

"Chile, I don't know. Be a new little boy in and outta that house every week," Mary Anne responded.

"You think he dealing drugs?"

"He sho' is, girl. And they say he good at it, too. That nigga could sell dick to a dyke."

"Girl, you crazy," Betty Mae said with a laugh. "So, he really *is* selling drugs?"

"Yeah, but I think it's more than just selling drugs."

"What you think he doing, Mary Anne? You know something I don't?"

"Well, you see all them feminine boys he bring home. Be switching like little women. I think they a bunch of punks."

"You think they gay?" Betty Mae leaned forward.

"Sho' nuff, they gay. Look at the way them sissies he bring be walking. And he try to sneak them around back. They still go to the front to get they cars out the driveway, so they ain't hiding nothing. Them dumbass niggas." Mary Anne laughed.

Barkley and Galaxy saw the two women on the porch. Barkley acknowledged them with a wave before Galaxy followed suit. The sight of them instilled fear in Barkley that he attempted to shrug off. He knew they had their suspicions about everything his life entailed, from his shady occupation to the company he kept. But he loved them anyway, especially Mary Anne, his former godmother. Disappointed and angered by the agony he caused her deceased best friend (and his grandmother), she quit playing the role of godmother a long time ago. Contrary to what Barkley thought, it had pained Mary Anne to disown him.

"How you doing, Barkley?" Betty Mae asked.

"I'm all right, Mrs. Jones. Y'all okay?"

The women nodded and watched the two men step onto the front porch of Sarah's old house.

"Look at them. Justa smiling. They don't know they going to hell."

"Mary Anne, shut your mouth."

They chuckled as the front door to the house across the street closed.

When Galaxy had lifted his frail arm to wave at the two women, Barkley worried about what they thought. He was glad Galaxy stayed quiet because he didn't want the women to hear his boyfriend's delicate voice. Having barely glanced at them (one of whom he would've remembered from Leroy's Corner Store), Galaxy didn't slide any of his concern their way. His life had taken a turn when he moved in with Barkley the previous week. Galaxy misjudged the gravity of the situation into which he had gotten himself. He didn't know whether this was an act of love or desperation. He would never know why he chose this situation instead of renting a home somewhere else. Fortunately for them, Galaxy had let go of reservations by giving up the luxuries to which he was accustomed to take a chance on love.

A fierce bond had already been restored between the two men, and that connection would strengthen. Barkley had been lonely in that house, and Galaxy would be the person he could hold during the long nights. This relationship called for more than the sexual ties they had developed. They needed further information about each other so their rapport would outlast its once-spontaneous nature and become as sturdy as the house in which they now lived.

That house, and every structure in Mansaville, was about to endure the roughest storm they had experienced in years. It started with a howl that somehow seemed louder inside than if you were to step outside to have a listen. But only a foolish man would have done that because the winds of the Confederacy would have knocked him over, and the blood pouring from the sky would have blinded him.

Upon hearing the eerie cry, the women of Mansaville—especially those on the factory side of the river—rushed out back to get their clothes off the lines. The men ran about their houses, closing all windows and locking doors once their loved ones were confirmed to be inside. Closing the windows didn't prevent the smell of death from coming out of the river in a fog that rose to the height of the trees. The haze would descend to envelop the whole town in the devil's stench of hate.

On the front of Old Scratch's raft lay the body of a two-year-old girl he had abducted and stabbed to death. He wasn't totally heartless, though, since he had made plans to return the dead body to her parents' doorstep with his favorite knife still in her back. Today, Old Scratch had been inspired by his act of pedicide, so he paddled across the Confederate River ever so slowly as the bones rose up to the surface of the bloody water. Some of the skulls appeared to smirk as blood fell upon them from the heavens they would never reach. Wearing a red mask covering the left side of his face, Old Scratch, cloaked in a black robe, stuck out his tongue to taste his work. The flavor was so deliciously wicked that he smiled just before waving his hand to summon his followers.

The skeletons listened.

They always took heed of their savior.

The remains of Confederate soldiers, as you may well remember, dwelled in the river. Many years ago, the devil had called upon them once he realized Mansaville was a thriving town. Now, he signaled with his hand to beckon them again. With each flick of his wrist, more skinless, organ-deprived bodies emerged from the water.

Some intact.

Others dismembered.

All of them floated repulsively, for they were the bones of Confederate soldiers!

Then came the loudest thunder ever heard, accompanied by lightning that zigzagged across the sky. Liberty Baptist Church's façade changed from white to a disgusting pink as the devil's tears rained upon it. Mister Tree's branches swayed back and forth, revealing him to be the origin of the wail, for the wind was shaking the lynched souls that stuck to his branches. The sky darkened as bloodshot clouds paraded across it.

Down the street, after having dismissed Betty Mae, Mary Anne looked out of her window, proud of what her son was doing. Her breasts filled with blood because she desperately wished to nurse her porcelain-toned child, the most beautiful murderer in the land.

Inside Grandma Sarah's house, Barkley and Galaxy held each other as they lay on the bed.

"You good, little man?"

"No." Galaxy put his face against his boyfriend's chest.

"Don't worry, baby. I got you," Barkley said.

He later dozed off, still holding Galaxy.

Had Barkley stayed awake, he would have realized Galaxy was the Protector. He would have witnessed blue sparks flying out of Galaxy's back. Instead, he saw flashes of lightning when the thunderous sounds of the Confederacy woke him well after Galaxy's fire had stopped. It was clear the storm envied an earthquake because its rumblings were so loud the ground shuddered, as did the houses, causing windows to rattle. All of this transpired because of a devil who was raised in a body of water flowing with blood. Though his power was imagined, people afforded authority to him because they bought into his false teachings, making his strength as real as the slave blood that kept his raft afloat. Unbeknownst to everyone in Mansaville, the Confederate body of water was pretending to be a river, though it was really just a brook.

15

Two weeks after Galaxy settled in, he and Barkley relaxed in the living room. They sat side by side on the couch, a position that solicited no eye contact but one that called for touching. Their physical intimacy mirrored that of the soul-altering exchange they were about to have.

"I can't help but think this situation is a bit odd." Galaxy enjoyed the warmth of the hard body sitting next to him.

"So odd you gave me head?" Barkley asked with raised eyebrows.

"Your sarcasm is not cute."

"But I have a point, right?" Barkley asked.

"I guess so." Galaxy softened his voice in resignation. He gave Barkley a gentle elbow to the side. "I just think it's strange, is all. You know—moving in here after you were away for two years."

The silence they had once fended off interrupted their conversation. Barkley moved closer to Galaxy and put his arm around him. Though shrouded in vulnerability, Galaxy avoided putting his head on Barkley's broad shoulder.

"It'll work out, baby."

"I know, sugar," Galaxy whispered.

Barkley kissed his boyfriend on the cheek. "You're safe with me." There were layers in his voice that were innocent and strong.

By now, Barkley typically would have been more sexual, resorting to his fuck-tested game plan: taking off his shirt and making his pectorals move with a flex of his chest. For once, intercourse wasn't on his mind. Neither one of them realized they were sitting in the dark as Galaxy finally put his head on Barkley's shoulder. The ceiling light had gone out long ago. Having grown tired of stumbling and feeling around for things, Barkley had planned to change the bulb for quite a while, but as soon as Galaxy's head touched his shoulder, light seemed like a bad idea.

"You never talk too much about how you grew up. I know you're rich because you're a Goodfellow. You told me your momma caught you with a dude, but why would you give all that up and run away to this side of the river?" Barkley asked.

Galaxy took a breath and spoke about how his father had put so much pressure on him to succeed. He told of how his little sister, Michaela, was the product of an affair his father had. He then talked about how his mother took Michaela in and claimed it was an adoption to maintain the appearance of a perfect family. Lastly, he held back tears while relaying that his mother was an alcoholic who took her frustrations out on him.

With those revelations, the night chill had crept into the house and coaxed the two of them to sit quietly until Barkley uttered, "It's getting late, little man. You ready to lay down?"

Galaxy nodded his head. They got up from the couch and strode down the hallway to the bedchamber.

"I have to go to the restroom to freshen up," Galaxy said.

"We ain't got no restrooms in here, just bathrooms. How many times do I have to tell you that?"

Rolling his eyes, Galaxy tilted his head and faked a frown that disappeared when he reflected on Barkley's use of "we."

Barkley removed his clothes down to his boxer briefs and pulled the covers back on the bed. He made it a point to keep the heater turned off. Cool air called for cuddling, and he wanted to see what Galaxy felt like in his arms once more.

Galaxy came out of the bathroom in a white T-shirt and pajama bottoms. He regarded Barkley's sexy form. The muscles, the skin tone, the large hands and feet. The trail of thick hair traveling from just underneath Barkley's navel down to his well-filled boxer shorts.

After Galaxy found his spot in bed, Barkley rolled over and put his chest to Galaxy's back and wrapped his right arm around him. His exhales sang Galaxy a lullaby as a legion of clouds goose-stepped in the sky, sending down fierce rain. The two men wanted to say something, but they heard thunder and saw flashes of lightning. It wasn't the tempest of Confederate blood that came every month. This was a perfect storm, the good kind that cleansed the entire town. Barkley and Galaxy didn't speak while the cloudburst was underway. They just lay there in silence and let the Lord do His work.

16

When Galaxy awoke, the house had ripened into familiarity. It felt like home. Realizing his boyfriend wasn't beside him, he called out, "Barkley?"

No response.

"Barkley?"

Galaxy patrolled the house looking for him but eventually resigned from the fruitless search and went to the bathroom.

"Why didn't he at least tell me he was leaving?" he asked aloud.

The sound of keys brought instant happiness to Galaxy, who smiled as he heard the front door swing open.

"Did you miss me, little man?" Barkley held a bag of food in his hand as he leaned in to hug his little boyfriend.

"No, I didn't."

"Yes, you did," Barkley countered.

"Whatever."

"I brought food." Barkley held up the bag once more.

"Good, 'cause I'm starving."

Barkley smiled and put his lips to the side of his boyfriend's deep mahogany face. They sat and ate. One would occasionally glance across the table to see what the other looked like while chewing. They found joy in doing simple things together. With each other, they saw beauty in the banal and music in the mundane.

"You barely touched your food," Barkley said.

"I'm not as hungry as I thought I'd be."

"I'll take it if you don't want it," Barkley said.

Galaxy slid the food across the table and stared at the wall. He missed having eggs in a basket with chives sprinkled on top, along with a side of pancetta and dark roast coffee from arabica beans. He gazed at Barkley, an enigmatic man he loved so much.

"Barkley, what do you do for a living?"

"Don't play stupid, little man. You already have your suspicions."

"Yeah, I do." Nodding his head, Galaxy looked down at the table.

"Well, what you've been thinking is right," Barkley said.

Silence reintroduced itself as they made eye contact.

"You got a problem with that?" Never needing approval from anyone, Barkley had always been unapologetic about his means of generating income.

"I'm okay with it, as long as it doesn't have a negative impact on me . . . on us," Galaxy said.

"It won't." He reached across the table to grab his boyfriend's hand.

"You promise?" Galaxy asked.

"Yeah, baby, I promise."

With that pact, they got up and approached one another. Careful not to knock over unfinished food, Galaxy sat on the table as Barkley instinctively stood right between Galaxy's legs.

With closed eyes, Barkley leaned down and pressed his thick lips against those of his boyfriend, who held the sides of Barkley's face with his delicate hands. Their kiss whispered to one another. There was nothing like the lips of another man—that combination of soft and hard, radiance and dark, song and silence that screamed *love* above the whisper.

17

In the late thirteenth century, Mansa Musa, the future African king of the Mali Empire, was born in a small village. His community was the home of a sapphire crystal said to be worth more than all of the money in the world, and it had magical powers. Artisans had embedded the gemstone in a crown they kept in the center of the village. Every week they would hold hands and stand in a circle around the crown, not to worship it but to appreciate the treasure as a symbol of independence, prosperity, and good health. While the crystal glistened in the crown, the villagers would chant a song to the ancestors. It was a refrain of gratitude, for no one in the tribe had taken sick since the crystal had been present. The community would have continued to thrive if the gem had been kept a secret, but one villager told an outsider about the stone's existence.

Revealing the gemstone's presence to one white man led to hundreds of Europeans hearing about it, and they came to the village to kill everyone and steal the crystal. With the determination of conquering colonists, they succeeded in murdering all of the villagers, except Mansa Musa and his mother. He was just a baby, so his mother held him in her arms as she fled, having already taken the crown that held the stone. She ran as fast as she could, but the Europeans, well versed in pillaging and plundering, pursued her. She made it to a lake and stood on a cliff above it.

She backed up as if to jump into the water with the crown and the baby. Afraid the stone would be lost for good, the Europeans doused her with a flammable substance and said they would kill her and the child if she denied them the crown containing the sapphire crystal. They didn't know she had already used a knife to pry the gemstone from it. When she gave them the crown and they realized the crystal was missing, they set her and her baby on fire and threw the crown into the lake. As her body scorched, she said, "You fools," while showing them the stone. While still in flames, she put the crystal in her baby's mouth and jumped into the lake. When she and her child landed in the water, the lake itself turned into blue fire, fueled by the power of the sapphire gemstone. The flames rose up the cliff and consumed the colonists, killing them all in a blaze of rebellion.

All the while, a young lady from a neighboring village was standing by the lake. The woman didn't know she was bearing witness to the first fire-bathing ritual from which sapphire warriors were made, but she understood the importance of keeping the story alive, a task that was made much easier when she returned to the lake sixty-seven days later, only to find Mansa Musa.

There he was, the future baby king. Though his mother had perished, he was left unharmed, and it showed in his magical appearance.

He was glowing in the most beautiful blue light!

Mansa Musa shone because the sapphire crystal was a part of him. She took him to her village to present him to the tribe. Upon seeing the child, the villagers knelt, cried, and proclaimed him king.

18

Because of his bloodline and blue fire, Galaxy was Old Scratch's prime target. Galaxy was the only one of his kind living in Mansaville. He had been too busy focusing on being in his new home to worry about Old Scratch. He instead wanted to make Barkley's place feel more luxurious, like the home in which he was brought up. He focused on the bathroom, the space in Barkley's house that seemed to rise above its working-class existence.

Galaxy fell in love with the claw-foot tub in which he was now taking a bath. In a chair that had been dragged to the side of the tub sat Barkley, who had just placed an empty drinking glass on the floor beside it.

"Galaxy, I need to talk to you." His words came out like maple syrup, minus the sweetness.

"What's going on?"

"It's about something that happened a few years ago," Barkley said, his voice still possessing its maple slowness.

"Okay. What is it?"

Barkley made eye contact and let out a breath. "Years ago, when I was fucking you at a hotel, I saw something crazy happen."

"You saw my ass jiggling." Galaxy smiled.

"I'm being serious right now." He raised his voice but kept it much lower than a yell.

"Okay." Galaxy sat up a little more in the tub, his naked body visible now that the bubbles had disappeared.

Barkley continued, "I saw something shoot out of your back."

Galaxy's eyes widened. "What did you see?"

"Blue sparks. Every time I dug balls deep in that ass, sparks came out of your back."

"And you kept going?" Galaxy asked.

"Damn right, I did. A nigga was about to nut. Plus, I was high, so I kinda thought I was tripping. I let it go, but I saw it again last night while you were sleeping. I think you were having a bad dream."

Galaxy sighed and said, "I'm not supposed to talk about the fire."

"Well, it's out there now," Barkley said. "I know what the fuck I saw."

"You know how Mansaville is. Crazy shit happens sometimes."

"Yeah, I get it. The town is haunted. It rains blood, and the devil appears on a raft in the river. I know all of that. Everybody in town knows."

"So, what's the issue, then?" Galaxy shrugged his shoulders.

"I grew up knowing that other shit, but fire coming out of your back? I wasn't ready for that, little man."

"And you waited this long to ask me about it?"

"I told you I was high the first time I saw it. Plus, my grandma said when you see supernatural things, leave them alone before you wake up something you don't want to deal with."

"I get it," Galaxy responded.

"Tell me what's up." He patted himself on the chest.

Galaxy exhaled. "I really don't know that much about it."

"Tell me what you know."

"It's supposed to be a secret," Galaxy said.

"You should trust me by now." Barkley interlocked his fingers as if praying.

"I do trust you."

"Then act like it." He unclenched his prayerful hands.

"Okay." Galaxy's whisper was accompanied with another sigh. "I had a talk with my granddad a month before he died."

"Satchel Goodfellow?"

"No. Satchel's son. He called me into a room and told me some men will be born with blue fire that protects us."

"From what?" Barkley inched forward in his chair.

"I don't know. He said in order to find out, I had to attend Morehouse because of its legacy." Galaxy cupped water in his hands and splashed it on his face.

"That's all he said?"

"No." Galaxy took a deep breath and told the story of Mansa Musa and the sapphire crystal. When finished, he got out of the tub and said, "I'm sorry, sugar. That's all I know."

"It's all right, baby. That was enough," Barkley replied, his voice low.

Galaxy leaned over the tub to unplug the drain.

"Don't do that. I'll take care of it."

"Thanks." He kissed Barkley and marched out of the room.

Still sitting in the chair by the tub, Barkley picked up the empty drinking glass he had placed on the floor. He dipped it into the water, filling it up. Barkley then did something you should always do when you're in love: He drank his partner's bathwater.

PART V

The Order of Black Dragons

19

They say that ol' white house at the top of the hill had the best moon-
shine in all of South Carolina.
You know what house I'm talking about—
the great big ol' plantation house,
the white one with black shutters.

That's where the whiskey was—the whiskey they tried to keep black folks
from drinking. They say one sip would send you to a magical place.

No one knows what was in that moonshine that was in that house
down the dirt road and up the hill.

But they say over fifty years ago, everyone fought hard to get it—
fought so hard it almost tore the whole town apart.

The field over there used to have a saloon, a brothel, and who knows
what else. It's gone now—burned to the ground—all because they were
fighting over that moonshine, that good whiskey that burns your throat
and makes you wave your hands in the air.

Like I said, nobody knows how they made that moonshine.
They've kept that a secret for years.
I heard something about an old recipe they stole from a slave named
Percy Lee.
I guess a slave had to do something to feel like he had freedom.

They say Percy Lee made it after he got some lashes from his master.
The pain was so bad he had to come up with something to get his mind
off of it.

So, he got to thinking about a potion he could drink the next time he
got whipped—
he wanted something to make the sting of the whip feel like nothing—
nothing at all.
It took him some twenty years to get it right, but sho' nuff, he did.

And he was about to get rich,
but them masters found out,
tortured him 'til he told them the recipe to make it,
and they killed him right there.
Buried him behind that house down the dirt road and up the hill.
The house they tried to keep black folks out of.

When the slaves were freed, the white folks got scared.
So, they stashed all the moonshine in that house down yonder—
the one down the dirt road and up the hill.

So many done tried to get in that house just to get a taste of it.
Nobody ever got far.
They either got hanged,
beaten to death,
or got run out of town—never to return.
They say getting that moonshine was harder than anything anyone has
ever tried to do.

So, everyone used to dream about going down the dirt road and up the
hill to that great big ol' house, the white one with black shutters.
You know which house I'm talking about—
the one they tried to keep black folks out of.

But along came a young man named Satchel Goodfellow—he read books all the time and spoke right. And that scared the mess out of them white folks.

As the story goes,
Satchel wanted to get him a swig of that good whiskey,
so he took a stab at getting in that ol' house.

All the power in the world tried to keep the colored folk from getting in the house that was down the dirt road and up the hill.

Satchel didn't let that stop him from trying.
He was black as midnight and proud of it.
He was about thirty-four years old—
short for a man,
and skinny as all get out.
Good looking though.

On that day, he had on a pair of overalls with a red flannel shirt and a pair of work boots.

Satchel didn't care about what he was wearing—he just wanted a sip of that moonshine,
so he walked down the dirt road and up the hill to that house.

You know, the one they tried to keep black folks out of.

There was a white man in there—
he was forty-six years old,
tall, with a little weight around the stomach.

He saw Satchel coming, so he went to the door to try to keep Satchel out. Everyone in town knowed the locks didn't work, so leaning and pushing up against the door was all the white man could do.

So that's what he did, even before Satchel got there.

Satchel had finally made it down the dirt road and up the hill to that house.

You know which house I'm talking about—the one they tried to keep black folks out of.

Satchel stepped onto the porch and could hear the white man laughing. Satchel turned the doorknob and tried to push the door open. The white man was on the other side, pushing as hard as he could to keep him out.

Satchel just slowly stepped away from the door and walked over to one of the windows.
It was cracked open.
Satchel lifted up the window slow, so the white man couldn't hear.
While he was climbing through the window,
the white man was still pushing on the door.

Satchel was finally in the house!
You know which house I'm talking about—
the one they tried to keep black folks out of.

The white man kept pushing on the door, while Satchel tiptoed to the staircase.
He was so busy pushing on the door, he didn't know Satchel was right behind him.

GALAXY GOODFELLOW

Satchel just eased up the stairs,
looking back every now and then.

The white man was still pushing on the door
while Satchel was making his way up the stairs.

Satchel was tiptoeing so slow, it took him a mighty long time to get to
the top,
but he finally made it.

And there it was
in a shiny bottle on a wooden chair at the top of the staircase.

He picked up the bottle, sat in the chair,
and looked down at the white man who was justa pushing on the door.

Satchel Goodfellow just sat there and smiled
and started sipping,
sipping away . . . sipping that good ol' bootleg whiskey.

20

Nearly four decades after the founding of Morehouse College, its president informed Satchel he would be valedictorian. Himself a graduate of Morehouse, Dr. Henry Watkins also had a PhD in history. Now fifty-two years old, he had developed a potbelly, and speckles of gray hair adorned his temples. Satchel noticed this as he sat in Dr. Watkins's office, dimly lit by a fireplace.

"This is quite an honor, young man," Dr. Watkins said, just after pulling a cigar out of his mouth.

"Thank you. I worked really hard for it, sir." Satchel looked around at items in the office.

"And it paid off."

"It certainly did, sir," Satchel said.

"In a way you will soon understand." Dr. Watkins offered a faint smile.

Satchel, dressed in a borrowed suit, eyed the smirk and sat upright in his chair. "What do you mean, sir?"

Dr. Watkins opened up his desk drawer, retrieved an old book, and handed it to Satchel, who gazed at the brown leather cover with the words "The Order of Black Dragons" inscribed in lettering reminiscent of a historical text.

"What is this?" Satchel asked.

"Open it."

Satchel complied, handling it like a fragile artifact. A slip of paper fell out and landed on the floor.

"I'm sorry, sir."

"It's okay, young man. It happens every year."

Satchel picked up the paper containing instructions, which he read silently.

Dr. Watkins puffed his cigar. "You will need to follow those commands tomorrow."

"Yes, sir," Satchel replied without nodding his head.

"You are one of a select group of people who will be a part of the Order of Black Dragons, unofficially known as the Morehouse Machine."

"The Morehouse Machine?" Satchel asked.

"Yes, the machine. A fraternal order made up of Morehouse valedictorians." He placed his cigar in an ashtray.

Satchel's eyes opened wide upon seeing the fire burning at the end of the cigar. It had turned sapphire in color.

Dr. Watkins chuckled. "All of this is a secret, you know."

"Of course." Hoping his words were convincing, he spoke in a whisper as his heart raced.

"The consequence of revealing this will be your life," Dr. Watkins added.

Satchel tried to sit more upright but had exhausted his posture. With sweat forming on his forehead, he said, "I-I understand, sir."

"As you should." Dr. Watkins picked up the cigar, took another puff, and looked in the direction of the fireplace. He waved his hand toward it and blue fire consumed the logs.

He eyed Satchel's face. "You didn't flinch like most. Interesting. The sapphire flames usually scare people. They will be yours, too. Quite soon, I might add."

Satchel sat motionless, except to nod his head.† "So, what is the Morehouse Machine?"

---

† When Satchel was eleven years old, he saw a mob of white men throw his father down a well and laugh while their victim drowned. From then on, Satchel learned to hide his fear because he thought it had prevented him from saving his father. This allowed him to appear calm in Dr. Watkins's office. Only someone who had witnessed his father drown would be more afraid of natural water than supernatural fire.

"It's a group of black men who make things happen. We meet every year to discuss plans for dominion."

"Dominion of?"

"Atlanta, the South, the United States, the world." Dr. Watkins smirked again.

"How?"

"With intelligence, money, death, and fire."

"Death?" Satchel adjusted his tie.

"Yes, death. We kill racist white people in furtherance of black power."

"What?"

"Not all white people, just those who choose to cause us harm, especially institutional harm." Dr. Watkins held up his hand and made a fist. The flames from the fireplace subsided. "Do you really think President McKinley died of a gunshot wound from a white man? Well, he did, but the assassin was chosen by the machine. We showed him our fire and threatened to kill him if he didn't take out McKinley. When he saw seven men from the Order of Black Dragons all wielding sapphire flames, he was so scared he pissed himself. We kidnapped him and brought him to the Conclave."

"What's the Conclave?"

"You'll see it tomorrow. It's where the Black Dragons meet. It's the headquarters of the machine."

"Where is it?"

"Here at the college. You'll find out soon. Just be patient, young man."

"Yes, sir." Satchel looked at the cigar that was no longer burning. "You said you kidnapped the assassin?"

"Ah, yes. We kidnapped him and brought him to the Conclave. We encircled him. All Black Dragons were locking arms and chanting. Fire came from our bodies. That's when he screamed. Once he saw that, it scared him into obedience. We told him he would burn in eternal sapphire if he didn't do what he was told."

"And you told him to assassinate the president of the United States?" Satchel asked.

"Yes, because we thought his successor would be better for the black cause."

"Roosevelt," Satchel said.

"Yes. He was somehow progressive *and* racist, but he was the best option."

"I understand." Satchel looked down.

Dr. Watkins stood and walked around the desk. While putting a hand on Satchel's shoulder, he said, "Young man, they are after us. We do good work, but we're human. So they will get every one of us someday. We just need to have enough Black Dragons left to continue the fight. We'll win the war, but a lot of battles will be lost. Many have already been lost, but we must press on."

"Yes, sir," Satchel said.

"Now, make sure you read the instructions. They will get you to the Conclave to be received by the king."

"What king?" Satchel asked.

"You'll find out soon enough."

"Yes, sir."

Dr. Watkins reached out his arms, Satchel stood, and they embraced. The flames in the fireplace burned brighter and dimmed after he and Dr. Watkins let go.

"Hold on to the book. Guard it with your life. And good luck," Dr. Watkins said. "Remember the tenet telling you to show no fear of the supernatural. That will be a difficult thing to do in the Conclave, but try your best. And do as the king instructs. He means you no harm."

"Yes, sir." Satchel put the slip of paper in his pocket and clutched the leatherbound book while leaving the office. As he stepped into the hallway, the lights flickered, and a waft of fog entered. After making his way through the haze, Satchel reached the wooden staircase. Just as he stood at the top of the stairs, he noticed a man lurking at the bottom. The stranger donned a black cloak covering his face. Though his countenance appeared as a shadow, his eyes sparkled. Satchel went down the staircase as the eerie man made his way to the top. As their shoulders touched in passing, Satchel shivered, a cold chill running through his body.

Once he descended the stairs, Satchel turned around and looked up. The cloaked man stood there with his bright, seductive green eyes still suspended inside a shadow. Satchel swiveled, dashed toward the double doors, and twisted one of the knobs the same way Old Scratch would soon twist his knife in the back of Dr. Watkins.

21

At midnight, Satchel ventured outside and made his way to the obelisk that stood in a wooded area on campus. The thirty-foot-tall structure towered, its opal shining in the moonlight. It rested on a slab of granite that appeared to be two pieces, though it was just one. It, too, possessed a sheen that danced in the moonlight. As advised, he approached the column and pressed the large sapphire crystal attached to it. He jumped back when a blue spark sprang from the gem. The ground underneath him trembled as the pillar slid backward to reveal a thin stone staircase that coiled downward like a serpent.

He inhaled, inched forward, and exhaled before pressing his feet onto the first stair. The ground shook again as the shiny, black obelisk shifted to cover the entrance, allowing him no way to climb out. A rank, dusty smell forced him to grimace as he regarded lanterns of blue fire adorning the stone wall surrounding the staircase. Taking deep breaths the entire time, Satchel paced down the staircase, placing his right hand on the wall to guide him. The farther he went, the more potent the smell of dust became. After he descended sixty-seven feet to the bottom, the odor disappeared.

With the last stair behind him, in front of him was a large circular room with glossy black floors. Blue fire burned in the center of the space.

"Is anyone here?" Satchel asked.

"Yes. Come to the fire." Possessing a West African accent, the man had a deep, gravelly voice.

Satchel advanced.

"Closer."

Satchel continued until the fire brightened, forcing him to squint and turn away. "Who are you?"

"Look toward the fire," the voice instructed.

As the flames diminished, Satchel could begin to make out the silhouette of a man—six feet, three inches tall and muscular. Appearing to be about thirty-five years old, the man stood there as blue fire disappeared into his dark skin.

He was nude. The sheer size of his penis, girthy and long, battled the impressive dimensions of his scrotum that was a touch darker than the rest of his genitals. His thighs were large and thick with visible definition as he stepped forward, his penis swaying as his thighs pressed against it, each testicle moving in unison with its corresponding thigh.

"Are you the king?"

"Yes, I am."

The king approached and put his hands on Satchel's shoulders.

"It's time for the Great Ritual."

"The Great Ritual?" Satchel asked.

"Yes. When you receive your fire and become a Black Dragon, a gear in the machine," the king said.

"The Morehouse Machine?"

"That's the unofficial name, but yes." He removed his hands from Satchel's shoulders and said, "You must disrobe."

Satchel took the orders and clenched his fists to conceal his shuddering hands. He was now naked.

"Follow me."

The king turned around and took deliberate steps. Satchel followed. They made their way past the area from which the king had emerged and stopped in front of a gray stone table.

"You are to lie face down." The king patted the granite, blue sparks flying from his hands.

Satchel complied.

The king rubbed his palms together, creating more blue sparks that he sprinkled on Satchel. Sapphire flames engulfed the king's hands. Satchel perspired, though the table and the sparks were cool to the touch. With this, the fear he had tried to suppress attacked him. His hands quivered.

"Don't be afraid. This is part of the sacrament. I must cleanse you."

"Okay," Satchel said before adding, "I meant, 'Okay, sir.'" His voice cracked.

The king laughed. "It's okay. Just relax and enjoy the flames."

He bathed Satchel, who closed his eyes and moaned in pleasure. With every motion of the king's hands, the flames intensified. The chill of the fire was soothing. The king massaged the flames into Satchel's skin. He rubbed both of Satchel's thighs, moving the fire slowly across the buttocks, back, shoulders, neck, and head.

"Turn over."

Satchel did. The king then washed the front of the young man's body, lathering Satchel's hair, chest, and stomach with flames. He massaged the sapphire into Satchel's penis, lifting it up to bring fire to all of it. He handled the scrotum with the same care. Then the front of the thighs and the feet. There was no arousal, just ritual.

"Get up and sit on the side of the table."

Satchel obeyed, his backside resting on the stone plateau, his legs dangling just above the floor. Sparks flew from Satchel's skin as the king held his hands above Satchel's head. The king released a firefall of sapphire onto the young man.

"Stand."

Satchel bolted upright as all of the flames in the Conclave disappeared.

The king grabbed the sides of his subject's face, looked down at him, and said, "Open your mouth."

Satchel did as he was told, for all his fear had been washed away in blue fire. Still holding the sides of the young man's face, the king blew fire into his mouth. Satchel breathed it in and exhaled crisp smoke from his nose.

"Did you memorize the oath?" the king asked.

"Yes, sir."

"You must recite it."

"Yes, sir." Satchel sighed. "I will fight the oppressor when challenged. I will defend my kingdom. I will reclaim what the white man has stolen. I will gain knowledge. I will support my people. I will maintain my domicile. I will be a Black Dragon whose fire will kill anyone who dares to destroy what I have built."

"And?" the king asked.

"I am superior, for I am a Black Dragon," Satchel said as his shameful nakedness turned into victorious nudity.

22

In the 1920s, Prohibition threatened to destroy Satchel's whiskey business and take away the money he would use to build Mansaville. In just under six years, he had assembled two small distilleries, a network of horse-riding distributors, and even three warehouses to store his liquor. He sold it to wealthy blacks in Atlanta, Charleston, and Charlotte. It wasn't just Prohibition that made him close the doors to one of his factories; it was the Ku Klux Klan. Satchel had been ready for them, especially in 1917 when they tried to take over his main distillery. The Klansmen, boasting eyes that looked like portals to hell, rode in one night and killed thirty-six of his employees, including two fourteen-year-old boys who served as runners. There had to be at least fifty of them, all white men dressed in sheets and hoods. They had guns loaded with bullets that were earmarked for niggers. The head and neck were their targets of choice. The ones who preferred to see blood aimed for the latter; the lazy ones set sights on the former. Satchel, with no weapon in his grasp, ran to the middle of the distillery where he saw the dead bodies of his employees.

"You crackers got the wrong one," Satchel yelled.

The Klansmen chuckled at the sight of a lone black man shouting down an army of whites.

"You must be Satchel Goodfellow."

"Yes, the fuck I am. What's it to you, white boy?"

"That ain't the way to talk to your superior," the Klansman said before adding, "Tie this nigger up."

They strapped Satchel to a wooden chair in a large, open room.

Six of the men poured gasoline on him. Another six doused the factory with it.

"Now, let's fry this son of a bitch." They went outside to a crucifix one of the men had planted and set aflame. It was burning with red-hot intensity in the cold night. Another Klansman lit his torch by sticking it in the burning cross.

"I'll do the honors." He threw the torch toward the building in which Satchel was tied up. The gasoline caught fire and spread blazes throughout the distillery. In seconds, the structure was engulfed. The flames erupted like fireworks. The Klansmen held their torches up in celebration . . . until the flames changed from reddish orange to sapphire blue. The laughter stopped at the sight of an ocean-colored blaze. They heard a roar, one that could only be the sound of a wild animal, except it wasn't wild like the Klansmen themselves were as they basked in ignorance. The growl was the most beautiful sound of all, for it was the strength of the order emerging from Satchel's chest. The Klansmen stood by the cross, watching in fear—perhaps even in awe—as blue sparks flew from the roof of the building. The sapphire shot out of the front, landing on the cross to turn its red fire into blue flames.

"What the hell is going on in there?" one of the Klansmen said as he got on his horse, which bucked like a bull and threw him to the ground. The horses all fled, as did the whip-o-wills that flew in a flock so high the blue sparks couldn't reach them.

"What the fuck?" another asked as he watched his horse run off like the others, except the stallions didn't stick together like those creatures in the air.

Some call the birds whip-o-wills, but you might call them nightjars. Nonetheless, they returned and circled in the sky above the Klansmen, and like only a flock of nightjars could, they sang—not to you, not to anyone you know, but to the tiger. Yes, the blue tiger that had materialized from Satchel's body in a blaze of splendor.

"We got to get out of here. The nightjars are singing." Those fearful words danced from the cross-burning Klansman's mouth to the rhythm of the singsong that chorused from the nocturnal flock above.

With the structure collapsing in on itself, Satchel rode out of it on the tiger made of blue fire.

"Oh my God!" one of the Klansmen yelled as he stared at Satchel, whose smooth dark skin had been unaffected by *their* fire.

Satchel dismounted the blazing tiger and yelled, "Fuck them crackers up!"

A roar.
A singsong from the nightjars.
A crackling cross.
Running horses.
Another roar.
White supremacy be damned,
for the Blue Tiger has arisen!

The tiger jumped on the man whose torch had set the building on fire. In seconds, the flames destroyed the Klansman's white garments and devoured his skin and insides, exposing a skeleton. The tiger turned its head, and from its mouth blue fire spewed and took hold of the remaining Klansmen, burning their sheets and leaving an army of skeletons standing there with nothing—stripped of the white skin they believed made them superior. The tiger had revealed them for what they were: brittle bones possessing neither heart nor brain.

The tiger made another motion with its head, releasing more blaze that hurled toward every skeleton, enveloping the skulls before making each one let out a high-pitched cry for Old Scratch. They all fell dead—or rather, dead again—to the ground. The devil heard them and would later gather their bones to be tossed into the Confederate River.

Once he throws the last skull into the water, he will die as well. But that won't stop the devil because he will always be reborn. You saw it with your own eyes when you visited Mary Anne's house.

23

Years after he had stepped down as mayor of Mansaville, Satchel frequently threw lavish parties at his estate. He had decorated his home with dozens of paintings, many depicting jazz musicians and people dancing in nightclubs. The African American figures' bodies were distorted, with arms that were too long to be anatomically correct, as they leaned back in positions that weren't humanly possible. Fixed in a permanent dance, they appeared to be possessed as they listened to the saxophonist and the pianist and the dark-skinned trumpeter whose cheeks were filled with air.

Unlike the smoke-filled rooms of the oil paintings, the Goodfellows' ballroom was well lit, with people moving about as if time were a mere plaything and not the universal keeper of life. Though there was plenty of smoke, it never lingered; rather, it disappeared into the chandelier's light after exiting the ends of cigars and cigarettes. The food had been catered, lobster on a platter the silversmith had crafted for this affair. Other trays had salmon caviar that sparkled in a coral hue. Brie and cold cuts rested atop what seemed like a twelve-foot-long charcuterie board made of wood similar to that of Mister Tree's storied branches.

None of the women were gauche, so their cigarettes had been carefully placed in black holders whose surfaces couldn't be felt on their gloved hands. Dressed in evening gowns with puddle hems, the women appeared to hover while their tuxedo-clad husbands guided them.

Satchel, having reached old age, could still dance with the best of them, as he and his wife did the Charleston to the beat of the live jazz band, which itself had been the finest in Mansaville. He led his wife through the ballroom. She upstaged him, somehow managing to do the shag in a pair of heels. The crowd smiled and applauded in appreciation of her moves. But unfortunately, Old Scratch made sure it was the last time she would ever dance because he taught her that even the most expensive champagne tastes as cheap as hell when it's laced with poison.

24

In December of 1965, Satchel Goodfellow lay in his hospital room in Charleston, South Carolina. He had been vacationing, something he had done just six times in his eighty-two years of life. While on the beach, two months after having buried his wife of fifty-four years, he felt tiredness in his arms, followed by shortness of breath and chest pains that forced him to fall to his hands and knees. His three sons ran to him.

"I'm fine. I don't need no help." Satchel grabbed his chest.

"I'm calling an ambulance," one of his sons said.

"At least send me to the Negro hospital so I can get the best care." Satchel attempted a yell that was just a whisper.

In defiance, his kids had him transported to another facility. While in the waiting room, Kenny (his oldest son) asked the doctor for a briefing.

"He had a heart attack, but he's okay now," the doctor said.

"So, he'll make a full recovery?" Kenny asked.

"Because of his age, it will take a bit longer, but yes, he'll be a hundred percent." The doctor smiled.

"Praise Jesus," Kenny said as he looked toward the ceiling.

The doctor laughed, covering his mouth to keep them from seeing his smirk.

"Thank you so much, Doctor." Kenny held his hands together. "I never got your name."

"My name is Doctor Scratch."

"Okay."

"Y'all should go on and get some rest. I'll make sure he's well taken care of," Dr. Scratch said.

"Yes, sir. We can sleep better now."

"You certainly can." The doctor snickered again but failed to cover his mouth this time.

As the sun outside appeared to descend into the Atlantic Ocean, Old Scratch made his way to the patient's room. Satchel watched him enter. When seeing the doctor's green eyes, he sat up as best he could and tried to scream. But a black serpent had slithered from the headboard and wrapped itself around his mouth. Blue fire emitted from Satchel's body. His sapphire had waned over the years, though it still had enough force to push Old Scratch to the floor.

"You arrogant old fool," Old Scratch said as a spider jumped out of his mouth. Possessing dark gray fur and a large abdomen, it crawled to a spot above Satchel's heart. It used its legs to cut a slit in the hospital gown and make an incision in the skin above the old man's ribs. The spider went inside Satchel's chest, wrapped its legs around his heart, and squeezed the life out of him. The serpent then relaxed its grip from the mouth of Satchel's dead body and slinked away. The slit in the gown disappeared, as did the remains of the spider that died from the blue flames of the old man's heart. Satchel had never been one to go down without a fight. His last thought: *This never would've happened if they had taken me to the Negro hospital.*

⟨∞⟩

Three days after Satchel's death, Mary Anne went to the wake to view the body. It was the first time she met the father who had shut his eyes to her existence. She reached into the casket and straightened his tie while fighting back tears.

"You trifling son of a bitch," Mary Anne said, smoothing out the maroon tie with the back of her right hand.

With those words, the dark flesh on Satchel's body decayed, exposing bones. The stench forced Mary Anne to step back before she reassumed her position close to his suited remains. To her, it wasn't a body. It was a corpse. As the wind howled and blew a gust through the funeral home, Satchel's flesh morphed into grains of sand, except for the eyelids, which opened to reveal surprised but dead eyes that became small mounds of sand themselves. At this, Mary Anne laughed while putting her fingers in the sand. After spitting on a handful of it, she threw it on top of her father's bones. The skull unbolted its mouth and whispered, "I'm sorry, Mary Anne."

The blinking eyes of a dead man hadn't fazed her, but his posthumous remorse made her scream and race out of the funeral home. All the while, her son—Old Scratch—sat in the corner in a cloak of darkness, a red mask covering part of his face.

Four days later, the funeral took place at Liberty Baptist Church. Mary Anne, having attended the public memorial, hadn't been invited to the private ceremony where her husband (who also didn't attend) was asked to allow a guest preacher to give the sermon. Poor Mary Anne wouldn't be there to sit with the Goodfellow family, whose blood she shared. There would, however, be an empty space between two of Satchel's sons, as if they knew Mary Anne should be there, though they had no idea she was their sister. The sons inherited the estate. She received nothing . . . not even the satisfaction of knowing that Old Scratch her demon son—was the one who murdered her father.

PART VI
The Baptism

25

My momma was a good woman up to the day she died. She would take me and my brother, Blacky, for long walks. We'd bring some of her good tea to drink and some fatback to snack on while we walked the trail. I tell you, she knew how to make some good fatback. The soft part wasn't too salty, and the skin crunched right.

Momma taught us so much. Taught Blacky how to love his dark color. I already loved mine, so I didn't need no teaching. But she did show me how to sew up a good dress. I 'member when she let me pick out some fabric for a dress she was making. I picked this real light orange material that had little purple flowers on it. Momma loved it as much as I did. She told me she was gonna use it to make the prettiest dress in Mansaville. And she was right. It turned out to be the most beautiful one I ever seen. She worked for over a year to get it to look the way she wanted. Momma put it on one day and showed it to me and Blacky. I tell you, she looked like an angel. When she was walking in it, it seemed like she was floating, and the dress looked like the wind was blowing it around. God musta helped her make it 'cause it was something you could wear in heaven.

Momma told me and Blacky she was waiting for the right time to wear it. She folded it up right neat, put it in a box, and tucked it away. Years had done gone by, and Momma never put it on. Then she died of 'monia. The doctors said her lungs got infected 'cause they had done filled up with fluid. So she never got a chance to wear the dress to town. That's why we had her buried in it. That made the best clothes in the world turn into the saddest outfit because a dress don't flow in the wind when it's inside a casket. You better 'member that. And 'member to stop holding on 'til the right time come. Any time is the right time to be your best. Don't wait to wear the good you. Put the good you on all the time. And don't be studying what other folks think. What you wear is your business. Long as you like it and the Good Lord like it, put it on. Ain't no point in having a pretty dress if you just gonna leave it in the closet.

26

When Grandma Sarah was seven years old and living in Atlanta, a christening gown was made just for her. It was the same orange hue as the dress in which her momma was buried, but instead of purple flowers, there was white lace. They took a spring pilgrimage to Sweetwater Creek, just west of the city. The reverend reached into the stream with a metal cup and scooped up some of the cool water. "Bless this child," he said before dipping his fingers into the cup and sprinkling some Sweetwater on Sarah's forehead. Her momma cried because her child had been baptized in the Methodist tradition. They didn't do it the way Baptists did by submersing you in water three times. Methodists were simple. They used sprinkles of water, yet the feeling was just as soothing.

Now, in Sarah's old house in Mansaville, Galaxy's presence soothed her grandson Barkley like the coolness of Sweetwater Creek. Galaxy had become used to his new life, even venturing out by himself on occasion to buy groceries for the house. During the day and for most of the night, Barkley was absent, forcing Galaxy to occupy himself with domestic affairs. Beautifying the house was his first order of business. Barkley thought it was appropriate for Galaxy to add his own style to the home.

Galaxy realized Barkley made plenty of money on the trap. He gave Galaxy carte blanche to redecorate and renovate the house. Though Barkley was unsure how his grandmother would have felt about his new arrangement, having her old home fixed up was his way of paying homage.

Hardwood floors were put down in the small kitchen in place of brown linoleum. The counters and cabinets were refinished, the latter with a maple varnish. New fixtures for the sinks were added. Galaxy had the shabby wallpaper replaced with a coat of beige paint. Thinking the kitchen was where he would spend a good bit of his time, he had wanted to upgrade it first.

"Shouldn't we have started with the bedroom?" Barkley asked.

"No, the kitchen is more important. Why fix up a room you can't even appreciate? All you do in there is sleep."

"We do more in it than sleep."

"I guess you have a point." He kissed Barkley and wrapped his arms around him before adding, "We'll fix up the bedroom, too."

"I'm just fucking with you, little man. You can do whatever you want."

"Okay, but there's one problem, though," Galaxy said.

"What, baby?" Barkley asked.

"I'm spending a whole lot of your money."

"Our money," Barkley said while placing his hand on Galaxy's shoulder.

"Well, our money. The problem is you never said anything about a budget."

"There ain't no budget, little man. I got plenty of paper," Barkley said.

"I just don't want to ask you for too much."

"It's cool. I like spending money on my bitches."

Galaxy found that word fitting because of the submissive nature it bestowed upon him. Even more than that, it was romantic. But Galaxy hated that Barkley made the word plural since Galaxy wanted to be the only one in his boyfriend's life. Until then, the thought of infidelity had escaped him. *Is this relationship official?* became the question that would loom in his psyche all day until it would dawn on him that moving in with Barkley, sleeping in his bed, and redecorating his house made it official.

He showed Barkley how much more he could spend by having the exterior of the house painted a soft yellow accented with green shutters. Out with the metal bars on the windows. "It's a small castle, not a prison," Galaxy told Barkley, who found humor in the comment. Without reservation, Barkley agreed, so long as he remained the king of that small castle on Church Street.

But Barkley did have doubts about upgrading the house when Galaxy enhanced the yard with an assortment of flowers. Galaxy carried out the plans despite knowing Barkley didn't want anyone to see a feminine boy in the yard. Barkley failed to realize people were already wondering what was going on at his place. Though it took most of them a while to notice, the townspeople reached the consensus that Barkley was in a romantic relationship with another man.

Residents of the factory side welcomed Galaxy's presence. It made for interesting conversation involving locals and not television characters or sporting events that none of them had the money to attend. Galaxy's arrival revitalized town gossip like never before. Some were intrigued by his pedigree (or rather, the idea of a Goodfellow living on their side of town). Others were put off by his effeminate nature. Even still, they were riveted by Galaxy and therefore wanted to know everything about him. But they were afraid to question Barkley, the man whose actions they wrongly believed had led to the death of his father. If Barkley had tried to kill his own flesh and blood, what would he do to someone who accused him of being gay? Even his best friends, Paul and Tyrone, let intimidation suppress inquiry. Barkley always told Paul the intimate details about his relationships with women, and Paul, who once shared a kiss‡ with Barkley behind Liberty Baptist, wondered why he refused to discuss this wealthy boy who had redecorated the most lucrative trap house this side of the Confederate River.

Tyrone, however, would never agree with having a friend who

---

‡   As you may remember, this is the kiss that Grandma Sarah witnessed. Though it happened years ago, neither Barkley nor Paul had ever spoken to each other about it, choosing to pretend it didn't mean anything—or worse, pretending it had never happened at all.

engaged in homosexual activity. That went against everything he believed manhood was. As soon as the rumors were the least bit plausible, Tyrone convinced himself that Barkley was no longer his friend. Never mind the lifetime they had known each other or the countless instances they had taken the fall for one another, Barkley was dead as far as friendship went. Now, all he was good for was business. Believing Barkley would go into a fit of rage, a fearful Tyrone would keep his thoughts and questions to himself.

But Mary Anne, the boldest person in the community, wasn't scared of Barkley; it was he who was fearful of her. Because she had been his grandmother's best friend, her opinion mattered a great deal to him. His sentimental side wished she would have reached out to him in his grandmother's absence. But she brushed him off, rolled her eyes when seeing him, and waved at him as though her hand were weighed down with iron. His deteriorating relationship with her saddened him, though he believed deep down that she still loved him.

Realizing that hiding forever wasn't an option, he knew there was something about Galaxy that was worth the risk of losing friends and having his reputation questioned by the entire community. Barkley now understood it would be impossible to maintain the down-low lifestyle. He would have to come out of the closet sooner or later, and taking Galaxy in had been the first step in making the shift. Barkley grasped that the process would be difficult, but he had no desire to go back to single life. He now came home to a clean, well-appointed home, and he had become accustomed to having a warm body in bed with him while sleeping. Someone to hold, keep warm, and defend. Barkley resided with a boyfriend who was attractive, intelligent, and submissive.

Love was now more important to him than superficial things because he was a drug-dealing rapist with values.

27

Just after the seventh week slinked in, Galaxy had the talk with Barkley for which they both had been waiting. On Friday of that week, Barkley had also crept in with red in his eyes and the dizzying smell of marijuana on his person. Galaxy had stayed up that night and was watching television when Barkley entered the bedroom.

"What are you doing, little man?" Barkley asked.

"Looking at videos."

"You don't have to wait up for me every night." Barkley stood in the doorway as he flicked the light switch.

"I hate when you do that," Galaxy said, grabbing the remote and turning off the TV.

"I can see you better with the lights on."

Galaxy peered at Barkley, who wore the sexiest outfit he had ever seen a guy wear. It was a mannish combination of a dingy wifebeater and a thin pair of red wind pants through which Galaxy could see the darkness of Barkley's legs.

"Why are you back so early?" Galaxy asked with a smile.

Barkley strolled to the bed, leaned down, and kissed his boyfriend.

"You smell bad," Galaxy said, beaming again.

"Whatever." Barkley stripped down to his underwear and got in bed.

"Stop trying to cuddle with me. Take a shower," Galaxy said, hoping it was convincing.

Ignoring the request, Barkley mumbled and laughed while pointing toward the ceiling. Galaxy was unable to stop giggling at his boyfriend's antics. The silliness would soon stop when Barkley spoke again, his regular speech patterns coming back to their pre-weed iteration. His eyebrows moved closer together as he bit his bottom lip, eventually releasing the bite to take a deep breath.

"People been fucking with me all my life. You get tired of everyone trying to test you. All that shit you been holding in comes to a head, and you fight everyone who gets in your face. That's how you earn respect—by fighting motherfuckers back. Even if you lose, they'll think twice about disrespecting you the next time."

Though he was high, Barkley was able to tell of how he stabbed his father in self-defense, ran off into the woods, and slept against a tree. Before passing out, he also spoke of spending two years in prison for murder although the autopsy report showed it was a heart attack that had led to his father's demise.

"That's how my lawyer got me out," Barkley said as he closed his eyes.

As the wind blew chilliness into the air outside, Barkley's story somehow brought warmth to the room. Galaxy pulled the covers back to cool off and rubbed the top of his boyfriend's head. He loved Barkley even more as he thought about the events Barkley had just recounted. Though Galaxy had already known about the assault because it had been reported in the newspaper, hearing it from Barkley made it feel real.

No one—not even Barkley—would ever know the medical examiner had found a large dead spider that had wrapped its legs around the heart of Barkley Sr., having squeezed the blood-pumping organ down to half its original size. The coroner said it was a heart attack, for he knew not what to call the evil deeds of one Old Scratch.

28

Galaxy was well acquainted with loneliness, but his new home possessed little to distract him. He had grown tired of watching television, though he would look at it every now and then. In dark hours like these, he would contemplate his own death. But, before his depressive thoughts got too far along, Barkley would come in and kiss them away.

One afternoon, when Barkley was available to give him one of those kisses, Galaxy had a deeper desire to want to know more about Barkley's mother. Galaxy had been down that long, winding road of telling Barkley almost everything about his life as a Goodfellow (from his rocky relationship with his own mother, to the untimely death of his father, to the time his mother walked in on him having sex with Old Scratch). But Barkley, having never been one to volunteer information unless he was drunk and high, was tight-lipped about his childhood.

Sure, he had talked about knifing his father. He had also discussed his time in prison. Those were things of which he was proud. The sentimental side of Barkley had yet to surface, and asking about his mother, Galaxy thought, would bring different emotions out of his boyfriend. Barkley enjoyed hearing about the colorful facets of other people's pasts, but when it came to his own background, he often used a dull, monochromatic palette and painted with sparse, unaffected strokes.

Galaxy made it his mission to change that when Barkley, wearing only gym shorts, paraded into the living room where Galaxy sat.

"Morning, little man. What are you doing?" Barkley asked.

"Reading a book by Jermain L. Reeves. He was a friend of mine."

"Was?"

"Yeah. He's gone now. He died fingering his asshole while skydiving. It felt so good he forgot to release the parachute."

Barkley shook his head. "Damn. That's fucked up."

"Yes, it is. I really miss him. He was a literary genius." Galaxy placed a bookmark in the novel's gutter. "Anyway, I've been wanting to ask about your mother. What was she like?"

"You mean what *is* she like?"

"Oh. She's still alive?" Galaxy closed the book and set it beside him. "So, what *is* she like?"

"A bitch."

Galaxy's brooch fell from his blouse.

"Not the answer you were expecting?" Barkley asked.

"Not really." Galaxy managed a soft chuckle.

"Truth is, I don't really know her. Wasn't around much. But I guess you know how that goes." He shrugged his shoulders.

"She wasn't around at all?" Galaxy asked.

"No. I can barely remember what she looked like. They say she just ran off and never came back. But I didn't miss her because I had my grandma." Barkley looked at a picture of Sarah and wanted to pick it up with both hands but decided against it and stared at Galaxy instead.

He finally accepted he was in love with Galaxy and had no regrets about it. Life was brand new to him. He wasn't just out in the streets hustling for the sake of having more money to buy expensive things. Barkley now worked to provide for Galaxy, a man richer than he.

"Well, little man. I got to go and get back out on the grind."

Galaxy folded his arms and marched to the kitchen.

"Baby, what's wrong?" Barkley slanted his face as he followed Galaxy.

"You already know what's wrong. You leave me here all day and half of the night, locked up in here like some animal." Galaxy stretched his arms as he spoke, his voice louder, eyes wider.

"Locked up? You go to the grocery store. You go for walks. What are you talking about, little man?" He, too, spread his arms.

"I came here to be me. Not to keep hiding," Galaxy whispered as he relaxed his posture.

"It ain't gonna be like this forever. I just—I just got shit to deal with."

"Well, deal with it. Whatever 'it' is." Galaxy turned away. "I know what the real problem is."

"What?" Barkley asked.

"You're embarrassed of me. You try to hide me so they won't find out about us." He spun around and made eye contact. "You think they aren't already talking? Well, they are, and I'm sure they've figured everything out by now."

"See, now you're tripping." Barkley waved his hand as if dismissing a child.

"Wake up! They've seen me out in the yard watering flowers. They've seen me at the store. They've even seen my car—you know—the one you try to hide as if they won't see it back there. Trust me, they've already put two and two together."

"How can they see you? I make you do everything when the sun goes down," Barkley said.

"Oh, please. That's when niggas come out. Besides, I don't like that you said 'make me.' You don't *make me* do shit." He wagged his index finger.

"That ain't what I meant," Barkley responded, shaking his head.

Arms folded, Galaxy asked, "Well, what do you mean?"

"All right, little man. Let me explain." Barkley paced to the living room and sat on the couch.

Galaxy followed but remained standing.

"Come sit right here." Barkley patted his own thighs.

Galaxy pretended not to want to sit on Barkley's lap but eventually did. With Galaxy's bottom so close to the business end of Barkley's dick, it was difficult for Barkley not to get an erection. Galaxy acted as if he didn't notice.

"Talk to me, little man. Tell Daddy what's wrong," Barkley said.

"I thought I just did."

"Well, tell me what I can do to fix it," Barkley said.

"I don't have to explain everything to you, do I?" His voice leapt toward the ceiling. He took a breath and said in a calmer tone, "I'm just frustrated. I feel like you're ashamed of me. I know I'm not the most masculine man, but . . . "

"It's not about that. I like who you are. I love you and shit."

"You do?"

"I wouldn't be going through all this if I didn't. I'll be ready real soon. I promise. It's just gonna take me a little time." He put his arms around Galaxy's waist. "You wanna come to the barbershop with me this weekend?"

"Yes!" Galaxy shut his eyes and smiled as he reopened them.

His exclamation echoed as they stood up and gazed at each other. Though Galaxy's face was not adorned, Barkley pictured removing Galaxy's glasses before kissing him. Instead, after tilting his head on its axis, he simply held both of his boyfriend's hands, leaned forward, and placed his lips against Galaxy's. With faint dances of the tongue, the intimacy seemed to teleport them to an undiscovered paradise light-years from the Milky Way. But as they embraced, there was no need to explore the universe because the best Galaxy was nestled in Barkley's arms, right here on Earth.

29

Galaxy noticed the stares they received when he and Barkley entered the barbershop full of men (old, young, and middle-aged), talking about everything from music to politics to rumors that this person was pregnant by that person.

While getting his own weekly haircut and shave, Reverend Johnny Whitaker sat in his chair, with tissue paper around his neck and a black piece of slick fabric around him to protect his bespoke suit from falling hair. He noticed subtleties no one else did. Barkley had opened the door for his "houseguest" and had looked down at the fellow's backside as they stepped through the barbershop, both avoiding clumps of hair covering the floor.

"Hey there, boys," said the same elderly guy who was standing in front of Leroy's Corner Store the day Galaxy had arrived on this side of town. Galaxy's nerves were slightly relieved at the sight of a familiar face.

"What's going on, y'all?" Barkley said as he made his way toward a set of wooden chairs padded with pleather cushions.

"Nothing. Same ol' gig. Cutting hair and eating pussy."

They all laughed.

"Sorry, Reverend, but this is my shop. And I'm older than you, so I can say whatever the fuck I want."

They chuckled again. Even Galaxy giggled as he sat down. This caused Johnny to witness another gentlemanly act the ex-convict displayed for Galaxy: Barkley had stood until Galaxy was seated. The reverend smiled at the gesture. Once again, the other men failed to take stock of it. Barkley always welcomed such inattention with open arms, constantly engaging in a balancing act. What could he do to show love for Galaxy without raising people's eyebrows? The poor man failed to spot that people's eyebrows were already raised.

"Y'all, this is my homeboy, Galaxy."

"I know this little rich nigga. He's a Goodfellow." The owner of the barbershop looked at Galaxy and said, "I know *you* ain't coming up in here to get no haircut." He dragged out the word *you* as if singing and added, "You probably got a personal stylist."

They all cackled again. For a brief moment, Galaxy made eye contact with Reverend Whitaker, who responded with a slight smile. He appreciated the distinguished appearance of the reverend, whose gray hair was descending to the floor, giving depth to the layers of black hair that had been cut from the previous person's head.

Johnny (as well as a few others) was mesmerized by Galaxy's form. His face, Johnny thought, was flawless—all features perfect. The owner of the shop found an attraction as well—nothing sexual, but an affinity nonetheless, one he could never articulate. Others in the shop recognized Galaxy's beauty also. All this in a room full of men. If the rumors were true about Barkley and this young boy, deep down in that place of honesty withheld from others, the men in the barbershop understood Galaxy's appeal.

In an attempt to fit into this community, when the barber offered him a complimentary haircut, Galaxy accepted. Barkley was satisfied with this, for if they both received service, it would validate their coming together.

"Now, if you like it, you gotta come back, little fella, you hear?"

"Yes, sir. I'll definitely come back," Galaxy said.

"But you gotta throw some money at me next time. I got rent to pay."

Everyone laughed again.

The old man's wisecracks were his way of relieving tension. Being a barber for over thirty years made him a good judge of people's reactions. He had been analyzing his clients' facial expressions for longer than either Galaxy or Barkley had been alive.

"Now, what you want done to your hair?"

"I don't know exactly," Galaxy replied.

"You don't know? You ain't too bright, is you? I'll just fix the cut you already got."

Galaxy leaned his head back with laughter, enjoying this brand of wit, an insult-based kind of which he wanted to be a part, but he saved his comeback lines lest he offend anyone. All five barber chairs were full of people who were not what he had expected. They were refreshingly different. Comforting with humor and warmth. They cut their eyes back and forth at Galaxy to steal glances of the barber's work. Galaxy was glad to get a professional haircut for a change, not the makeshift trims Barkley had been giving him while he sat in a folding chair as Barkley—clippers and razor in hand—stood above him to show off the training he had received in the penitentiary.

Galaxy winced at the sting of the alcohol-soaked napkin the barber used to trace his hairline. When the pain subsided, the corners of Galaxy's mouth curled upward while he looked in the mirror. The smile was triggered by the haircut as much as it was driven by this moment. For the first time, he felt Barkley celebrated him. So, when the barber held the mirror in front of him, Galaxy beamed. If he were not agnostic, he would have thanked God.

Meanwhile, Reverend Whitaker was finished getting his trim as well. He was glad Galaxy was done before Barkley, so he could take the time to talk with the newcomer and get a feel for his demeanor. The reverend wanted to confirm what his gut had been telling him.

"Step outside with me, young man. Just want to chat with you for a minute."

"Okay," Galaxy replied before turning to the barber and saying, "Thanks for the haircut, sir. It looks great."

"You're welcome, young man. Take care," the elder responded, patting him on the shoulder.

Johnny held the door. Galaxy nodded his head and crossed the threshold. Trying hard not to stare, everyone carried on with their respective conversations, knowing all the while they would later ask the reverend about Galaxy. From the barber chair, Barkley had recoiled at how the reverend had accosted Galaxy.

"Hurry up with my cut. I ain't got all day," Barkley said.

His barber chuckled, mistaking the remarks for a joke while Barkley gazed through the window at Galaxy and the reverend, attempting to interpret their body language. Unable to decipher their movements, frustration filled him because he distrusted the leader of his late grandmother's church.

"Well, young man, what brings you to this side of the river?" Johnny regretted not asking Galaxy how he was doing, but the reverend knew jumping directly into his inquiry was the best strategy.

"I needed a change of scenery," Galaxy said while looking down at the sidewalk.

"We don't get too many people from the industrial side of the river coming this way unless they have to go through here to get somewhere else." The reverend stood in the fig leaf position, with both hands over his crotch. He made a fist with the hand sporting his shiny wedding band and covered its sparkle with the palm of his other. He asked again, "So, what brings you here?"

"God did, I guess," Galaxy replied in an attempt to deal the reverend a wild card. He never prayed, never mentioned God, but he felt religion an appropriate defense mechanism against someone he perceived to be a devout man.

"I can't argue with that." Johnny was taken aback, believing most people from the other side were heathens. He had lumped Galaxy into that group before ever meeting him. Ironically, the reverend and his wife Mary Anne had been planning to move there.

"So, you preach at Liberty Baptist?" Galaxy asked.

"Yeah. Sure do. Been there a long time."

"I'm sure you have," Galaxy said.

"How old are you, if you don't mind my asking? You eighteen, nineteen, right?"

"Twenty-one."

Hearing Galaxy's age was the confirmation Reverend Whitaker needed, finding oddity in Barkley's desire to live with a boy this age, although Barkley himself was only twenty-six.

"Oh, you're a young buck." Johnny stepped forward. "So, Barkley took you in, I hear?"

"Yes, sir." Galaxy looked through the window at his boyfriend, whom he wanted to come outside and stop the reverend's interrogation.

"So, how y'all come to know each other?" Reverend Whitaker asked.

"Well, it's a long story," Galaxy said.

"Got nothing but time. Today is Saturday, my man. I don't preach 'til tomorrow."

"I might have to hear one of your sermons," Galaxy said in what Johnny rightly perceived as an attempt to change the subject.

"Yeah, you should come on out. We welcome anybody."

The word *anybody* concerned Galaxy.

Johnny realized his poor word choice but knew it was too late to correct it without causing more damage. He was about to speak again as Mary Anne pulled up.

"Here comes my wife. We got two cars, but today we're just using one." Johnny rubbed his wedding band.

Like the blood she smelled, Mary Anne seeped out of her sedan and oozed toward Galaxy. While sitting on her porch, Mrs. Whitaker had only regarded him from a distance, so she viewed this as a prime opportunity to see him up close like she had done months ago in the corner store.

"How are you, young man?" Mary Anne asked, taking a white glove off before grabbing Galaxy's hand.

"I'm fine. How are you?" Galaxy felt warmth come over his body.

"Blessed and saved," she replied in a soft tone as she released the handshake.

Johnny squinted as he looked at his wife. He hoped Galaxy wouldn't notice. Galaxy did not. But he wondered why she was wearing a pair of white gloves despite the discouragement of the humidity and the sharp sunlight.

"Why are you living with Barkley?" Mary Anne asked, eyes tilted heavenward, head angled hell-bound.

Reverend Whitaker nudged her.

"He's an old friend." The warmth in Galaxy's body moved toward his closed eyes, blue fire drumming up in them.

"And by that you mean?" Mary Anne gobbled up decency just to shit out disrespect.

Reverend Whitaker grabbed her arm.

"Answer the question, young man." That's her wiping her ass.

Sensing the stench of hate, Galaxy opened his eyes that were now consumed with blue fire. Mary Anne gasped, clutched her husband's hand, and stepped back.

"What's wrong?" So focused on taming his wife, Johnny missed the sapphire.

The blazes disappeared. Galaxy rubbed his eyes, unsure of what had transpired. He had felt the heat, but hadn't seen the flames. Given Mary Anne's reaction, he should have known.

"Well, Reverend Whitaker and I have to get going." Her voice shook as sweat sheeted her brow.

Johnny peered at his wife. Then he turned toward Galaxy and said, "Well . . ."

"We have to go. Now!" Mary Anne reclaimed her vocal steadiness, squeezed her husband's hand, and rushed him to the car.

"Take care, young man," the reverend said, looking over his shoulder.

Mary Anne was the only person who could scream under her breath, and she did so with this: "I knew something wasn't right about that boy. A nigga ain't got no business with blue eyes."

30

Almost every Saturday after returning from choir rehearsal, Mary Anne and Betty Mae, wife of Deacon Jones, had discussions on the front porch, but now they talked almost every day out of a relentless fascination with Galaxy and Barkley's relationship. Mary Anne, the vicious one, bold and brazen. Betty Mae, the warm neighbor who never liked to meddle in other people's affairs. Despite that, she clung to her preoccupation with the couple across the street. Odd, she thought, how one boy, now confirmed to be a Goodfellow, could stop the flow of other men from coming in and out of that house. *Why did that poor little child walk with his head down? Some sin had to be going on in there. Or was it sin? If they love each other, why can't they . . . .* Words she would never say in the weekly meetings held at Liberty Baptist Church. And words Mary Anne would never want to hear from her close friend and neighbor.

Although Mary Anne and Betty Mae's friendship seemed strong, it was built on shared pain. They gravitated toward each other as a result of what they suspected (or knew?) about their spouses. Their bond was based on emotional and sexual rejection. The poor women yearned for intimacy because neither had given their husbands a pint of pussy in years.§

The two women saw themselves in each other, especially how they

---

§   "Pint of pussy" is a term used to denote a woman allowing a man to penetrate her vagina. The shortened version is "pint." Example: "Girl, did you let him fuck you?" Response: "Yes, I gave him a pint of pussy." Alternative response: "Yes, I gave him a pint." The term "pint of pussy" was coined by Jermain L. Reeves, a man who has never and will never get pussy because he has zero interest in it.

tolerated the late meetings to which they were never invited. Instead of fighting their men, Betty Mae would cry and attempt to pray her sadness away. Mary Anne's husband was almost always gone, so she had few opportunities to give him a pint. She would, therefore, self-gratify to combat her despair.

They all would have benefited from self-analysis, but they chose the emotionally expedient path that turned out to have long-lasting deleterious effects. Had they looked into their own eyes to see how their tears formed, they would have known the roots of their problems. They failed to realize that the origins of misery often come from within. If you examine your tears, you can see the reflection of your own face.

31

After church let out the following Sunday, Mary Anne and Betty Mae rode home together. For the first time in years, they had enjoyed Johnny's sermon, an exciting rant and rave from the pulpit that energized everyone in the room. Even Mary Anne was so moved she waved her right hand just above her head. She and Betty Mae dreaded leaving the church this time.

To prolong their good spirits, they sat down on Mary Anne's porch to talk. Usually, they would eat and have a beverage, but their cheerful mood left no room for refreshments. Just after getting comfortable, they observed Barkley and Galaxy, who stood in front of the house across the street. The two guys regarded the women from the corners of their eyes, not wanting to give them, especially Mary Anne, the acknowledgment of a simple wave despite having done so in the past.

"Oooh, girl, look at them. They look a mess," Mary Anne said.

"Child, hush. Let them do what they want to do," Betty Mae responded.

"Two grown-ass men shouldn't be shacking up. It's a sin and a scandal." She frowned and shook her head.

"Now you hush up, Mary Anne. You talking too loud. They might hear you."

"I don't give a shit." Mary Anne took off her crimson hat and placed it in her lap. "Girl, I been 'round this world over seventy years and faggots ain't never threw it in my face." The anger in her voice had the resilience of a cockroach.

"Barkley got him a cute little boy, though."

"I never said he was ugly, but what he doing is wrong," Mary Anne said.

"But he cute and wrong." Betty Mae smiled.

"Cute people go to hell too."

"Girl, you a mess," Betty Mae responded with a laugh.

"But there's nothing wrong with a good-looking man. If I was his age, I'd run across this road and give him some of my cat," Mary Anne said.

They both laughed.

"That's what he needs, Betty Mae. He probably ain't never had none. Some good cat will turn his punk ass right back to Jesus."

"You one silly heifer."

Mary Anne quieted for a moment, leaned back, and said, "Sarah ain't raise Barkley to be no sissy. She was a good woman. In the church and everything. She loved that boy with all her heart."

"Now, you right about that. Loved him 'til the day she died," Betty Mae said.

"It just tore her up when he went to jail. She missed him more than her own son."

"That's the truth. She liked to fell out when they sent him away," Betty Mae said.

"Sarah didn't even get to see him before she died. God rest her soul. I bet she rolling over in her grave." Mary Anne pursed her lips.

"Now hush up, girl. She would love that child no matter what he is."

"Knowing her, she probably would, but they're still disrespecting her by doing they business in her house." Mary Anne stiffened her posture. "Sticking his willie up that boy's ass and making him shit in the opposite direction."

"Girl, stop." Betty Mae chuckled.

"It's the truth. All that fudge packing they be doing. The Goodfellow boy is the one getting fucked. You can tell by the way he be switching. If you put your ear to that nigga's asshole, you could hear the ocean."

They slumped over as their laughter echoed throughout the covered porch. Mary Anne strained to see Barkley, who lingered outside. He was a blur without her wire-framed glasses.

Mary Anne sat upright in her wicker chair and said, "He ought to be shot."

There was that cockroach again, and it was much more resilient this time.

32

Galaxy knew he and Barkley would go to Liberty Baptist Church the following day at Barkley's urging. Though they had been to the barbershop together, Galaxy still thought Barkley was ashamed to be seen with him. Understanding how his live-in boyfriend felt, Barkley wanted to show Galaxy otherwise by taking him to church. Though he was not fully ready to come out of the closet, Barkley was prepared to let everyone see them together once again, so people could make their own interpretation about his relationship with Galaxy. He was well aware of what their conclusion would be and accepted it, so long as he didn't have to verbally acknowledge his identity or show Galaxy affection in front of them. It would have taken a near miracle for him to be so bold.

Barkley told Galaxy there was a surprise he would give him that night. Having grown tired of meaningless sex, Barkley was ready to make passionate love to his boyfriend. Galaxy must have had some idea of what the gift would be since he bathed thoroughly and sprayed perfume on his private parts, wanting his body to be perfect for his man. In the time it took for a season to pass, Barkley had taught him what true love really meant. Now, sexual intimacy would blow its seasonal winds and unite the two of them in ways they thought were impossible.

By nightfall, they were almost too anxious to function, and the silence in the air did little to comfort them. The television was off, and the usual sound of crickets chirping had disappeared, as did the rumblings of cars driving by their home. After having told all of his friends and associates not to visit, Barkley turned the ringer off the house phone, desiring only the rhythmic sounds of romance.

When they walked into the bedroom, neither could articulate his feelings, both wanting to express themselves under the warmth of one another and under the faint tickle of bed linens. They stood by the window, the curtain pulled back to allow the moon's glow to pour onto the floor. In this town in the middle of nowhere, they looked at the night sky and gazed at cities of stars. Barkley and Galaxy may have felt unchaperoned in Mansaville, but they were not alone in the ocean of existence. The realization of just being—of merely drawing breath—made them grab each other's hands, for they were the stars in this place.

Barkley had dressed the bed in white sheets. It was the first time since Galaxy's arrival that Barkley had taken on any type of domestic task that didn't involve cooking. He usually left the household chores to Galaxy. This time, Barkley wanted the young boy to rest and be taken care of like never before.

After Galaxy lay down on the bed, Barkley climbed on top of him and kissed his boyfriend, making sure the touch was soft and unhurried as he lorded over Galaxy, whose eyes calmed him. They had fucked countless times, but tonight would be the first occasion in which they made love. This wouldn't be the typical sex whereby a three-week courtship is distilled into a three-second orgasm. In its place would be slow, passionate lovemaking by dint of having forged a yearslong romance. They treated this as if it were their first time together because, in a sense, it was. The kiss just flashes ago was a fitting precursor to the coming moments.

"You ready?" Barkley found the words to speak.

"Yeah, I think so," Galaxy replied.

"It'll be better than ever because this time it's with me."

"I'm a little bit nervous," Galaxy said.

"Nervous about what? It's just me. I ain't the devil."

"I know." Galaxy looked up at Barkley. "I guess this is it."

"Yeah, I guess so."

"Two gay men making love to each other for the first time," Galaxy said.

"I ain't gay. I'm just a nigga in love with you."

Barkley unbuttoned Galaxy's top and kissed him on the lips with each unfastening, opening the younger man's black shirt to reveal a smooth chest moist with sweat as he explored every inch of that chest, tasting the sweet salt Galaxy's skin offered. With all of his garments molted from his skin, Galaxy remained on his back while being ravished. Barkley knew Galaxy's body. This gave him the power. He was strong and dominant, yet comforting and gentle, as he lay on top of Galaxy.

"Lie on your back, sugar," Galaxy said.

Barkley complied.

And they made music. It was much too slow to be hip-hop, much too old-world to be rhythm and blues . . . so it just had to be jazz because Galaxy was holding Barkley's saxophone, the wooden reed and mouthpiece ready to be blown. He grabbed the neck of the sax and tapped his fingers on the keys while blowing gently, causing the instrument to make a noise. As the saxophonist's mouth tired, he went rogue and introduced a harmonica to the arrangement. He moved around to the side of the device and slid it in his mouth from side to side in the way a harmonica is played. The music it made was just as intense, but it had moved from 1920s jazz to a modern 1990s version that was up-tempo and heavier on the percussion.

Though his instrument had been played many a night, Barkley had been waiting for this masterfully stylized song. This was a different experience. For once, like the tenors at Liberty Baptist Church, he took his time. It wasn't about exerting pain for his own gratification. It was about providing pleasure to a loved one. To that end, Barkley shifted Galaxy, hovered over him, and gave him a look as passionate as this scene is overwritten.

One masculine and on the top.

One feminine and on the bottom.

The contrast of their bodies evaporated in the darkness, and their distinction disappeared with eventual penetration. Together, they were making a song, its first lyric an alliterative one because their movement sparked beautiful blue blazes from Galaxy's back. The fire burned cold, soothing both of them. Lying face up, Galaxy couldn't arch his back, so he curved his chest instead, forcing—rather, guiding—their hearts closer. Beating in unison, their hearts provided the rhythm of love. Barkley's motions showcased the melody, while Galaxy's moans presented the harmony. Their eye contact, the direction.

As musical metaphor hushes into more purple prose, Old Scratch sits in the corner, smoking a cigarette, watching a powerful man make love to Galaxy. With every push of Barkley's body, Galaxy was tightening his arms around him, his legs wrapped around his boyfriend's waist. Barkley loved the warmth of Galaxy's thighs pressing against him, so he stayed there, unable to fathom a better position. His blinks were few, wanting to read his partner's facial expressions and stroke accordingly.

"Do you smell smoke?" Galaxy asked. His eyes sparkled in the moonlight that still poured through the window.

"No, little man. Just relax and let Daddy do his thing."

Barkley unleashed a suite of thrusts, the circular ones hitting the spot. Overcome, Galaxy wept, now believing that any man can fuck you, but only a black man's dick can take you to church. And that's what Barkley did. He deployed his dick to minister to Galaxy and to tap that ass with spirituality. He grew more in love with Galaxy, whose body was pure to the touch, making Barkley tingle with every caress. When the sensation reached an apex, he baptized Galaxy on the inside—not with much, but with sprinkles of his water—like the Methodists down at Sweetwater Creek.

When their bodies spoke, Barkley kissed Galaxy in the absence of penetration. Without uttering a word, the two men held each other. They knew it was time to stop hiding. Barkley, the more fearful one, understood the love they had just made wasn't the shameful kind. It was romance that should be celebrated. But their great reveal would come soon enough. For the time being, they would close their eyes and attempt to sleep the night away, for they were deeply in love and forever bound, like this novel.

33

The smell of cigarette smoke woke Galaxy up in the middle of the night. As his boyfriend lay there sound asleep, Galaxy saw Old Scratch (or more aptly put, saw him again). He slowly got out of bed, covered his King Barkley with a blanket, and drifted toward the world's most evil man. He looked at Old Scratch up close. Though the devil had fucked him before, this was the first time Galaxy realized what this man's appearance really meant.

The devil backed up, his cloak fell from his head, and his mask splintered as it hit the floor. This revealed Old Scratch to be a young man with dirty-blond hair, curly and soft. His eyes were green. His skin pale yet vibrant.

"You're nothing like me," Galaxy said in a whisper as he studied the devil's face.

With those words, Old Scratch's cloak tumbled from his shoulders and puddled at his feet. He was naked.

"You're nothing like me," Galaxy repeated.

A tear of blood dripped from Old Scratch's eye. Galaxy looked in the mirror, stared at himself, and said, "He's nothing like me."

The mirror shattered, and a shard of glass spun through the air, landing in Old Scratch's neck. Blood flowed from the wound, but he refused to die.

To the now broken looking glass, Galaxy proclaimed, "He's nothing like me."

Another sliver of glass hurled itself toward Old Scratch and struck him, leaving a vertical gash beside his left eye. As he hollered out, Old

Scratch—the devil himself—went from adulthood to puberty to a toddler to a baby crying for his older, more powerful self. The wound on his neck healed as he aged in reverse, but the scar next to his eye—the one that had blinked away the tear of blood—remained on his infant face. The cloak curled itself around him, the window opened, and the devil baby floated into the crisp air of the night, crying like only a fallen angel could. Scarred and scared, Old Scratch said, "Revenge is more fun than forgiveness," as the wind carried him away.

34

Though the weather was pleasant in all of Mansaville, a rainstorm was coming in the Whitaker residence as Mary Anne tried to stay quiet while her husband decked himself out for another evening away from home. Wearing a housedress, she stood in front of the mirror in her bedroom and peered at her facial wrinkles, one on each side, running from the bottom of her nose to the corners of her mouth. The skin under her eyes had thinned, giving it a sunken look, making her dark circles more prominent. Her once-perfect white teeth now had a yellow tone, appearing almost translucent around the edges where life's acidity had taken a toll on the enamel. She even had a few missing, though thankfully in the back.

After twisting her arms, she noticed that the skin on her elbows sagged. The sight bothered her to the point at which she remembered her demon baby, the one who kept her in perpetual motherhood. Mary Anne loved him for the semblance of youth he afforded her because a woman her age—at least a normal one—could no longer produce milk. She felt blessed to have a bosom that could nurse the beautiful green-eyed baby, the very embodiment of wickedness.

She dragged herself to the bed, pulled back the comforter and sheets, and tucked herself in. Blinking to keep the tears from showing, she rolled over to hide her face from her husband. This was the first time she had cried over Johnny in years. Mary Anne never could give him the satisfaction of seeing her tears. Though she knew her sadness didn't please him, concealing each drop of hurt was a small triumph because every defeat was gut-wrenching.

Mary Anne always wondered why he bathed in cologne just to do work at the church, but expressing those concerns would be to acknowledge her suspicion, which, in turn, could have confirmed her biggest fear. She took some comfort in knowing the woman in the house next door was in her own bed crying as the smell of Ray's cologne lingered in the air. When the tears dried, Mary Anne turned toward Johnny and found the courage to ask the question that had been sitting on the sour spot of her tongue.

"Where are you going this time of night?"

The reverend was taken aback by this inquiry and even more thrown by the pernicious way in which she gazed at him. His wife had never looked him squarely in the face when he prepared to leave into the night. Years and decades had passed without his hearing the question she had just posed. Terrified of further interrogation, the reverend lashed out at his wife.

He wagged his finger and shouted, "I'm a grown man. If I want to go out, I can go out!" Knowing he was showing his ass, he put his fisted hands on his hips and looked at her to gauge her expression.

"Don't raise your voice at me, Johnny." She pointed at his dick, not his face.

"I ain't raising my voice. I just said I'm grown." In pressed clothes, he still stood arms akimbo, his shirt missing the button he wanted to fasten to his wife's lips.

Silence. They stared each other down. He lost.

Pissed in perpetuity, Mary Anne had developed a knifelike voice. She slashed him with this: "You always go out in the middle of the night. You better not be cheating on me with some young little hussy. Even though you and I both know it ain't young, and it ain't no hussy, either."

Johnny swallowed and wilted. His wife exhaled.

"You think I'm a dumb bitch, don't you?" Her vocal knife dripped with blood.

"You talking crazy. It's just work stuff. You know I love you, girl."

He spoke in a castrated tone.

"I know, baby," she whispered.

Knife licked clean, Mary Anne distrusted words coming from a husband to whom she hadn't made love in years. But his sentiment still pacified her because she sensed sorrow in his voice. Knowing he felt some guilt for his wrongdoings proved comforting. Regret meant he loved her at least a little, and that sweetened the sour spot on her tongue.

"If I didn't love you, I wouldn't be building you that great big ol' house out yonder." Johnny grabbed his crotch to make sure his nuts were still attached.

Surveying his moon-damaged skin born of nighttime trysts, Mary Anne smiled as she pulled the covers up to her shoulders. Johnny hadn't professed his love for her since the beginning of their marriage.

"I won't be gone long," he said.

"Okay, I'll be asleep when you get here." Mary Anne hoped that would be the case. Seeing him come home and bathe saddened her.

"Okay, sweetheart." Johnny kissed her on the forehead and turned off the lamp. The soft pressing of his lips was just as foreign to her as "I love you," but she was desperately willing to become reacquainted with both, clinging to the false hope their marriage could be saved. She rolled over in their bed to block the view of him as he, without looking at her, squirmed out of the room. Now safe, Johnny threw a backward glance in her direction as if he could see through the wall. He sighed and made his way down the hallway and into the parlor. Then he left through the escape hatch faithful husbands call a front door.

Back in the bedroom, Mary Anne's egg-shaped eyes cracked to hatch tears denoting misery from which she couldn't escape. The weeping wife was left alone to cry herself to sleep, a true sign she had come to terms with the deterioration of her marriage. For this failed union, Johnny held most of the blame to be sure, but Mary Anne (like many) had closed her eyes the way she had as a girl when running into Mister Tree. She had clung to a fantasy that gave her solace, not a reality that would have afforded her power, for the very eyes she willfully shut were the same ones making waters of despondency fall down her face. It was hard for her to tell which was worse: looking at her own tears or feeling them roll southward on her countenance, their refractive properties magnifying the scar on which she still blamed Mister Tree, the sturdy oak that stood near the church.

But Johnny and Mary Anne's marriage was far from sturdy because it had been based on conceptual joy instead of true happiness. They, for different reasons, had been conditioned to believe they should get married young. Johnny and Mary Anne loved each other, yes, but in the way acquaintances cared about one another . . . or friends. . . or companions . . . but not lovers. Their romance was all so imagined, so synthetic and bereft of authenticity. They failed to understand that fake pleasure creates as much anguish as real pain, except the former causes you to rot from the inside, heart first. As she lay on their antique bed, Mary Anne's own heart seemed to beat a little slower as she listened to her husband's exiting footsteps, muffled by the rug under which rested a mound of secrets. He had spent decades trying to hide his sordid affair, and Mary Anne assisted in the cover-up by crafting an image of a perfect marriage. Their efforts were all in vain because the town already knew the truth about the filth they attempted to broom out of sight. That's why there's no point in sweeping dirt under a see-through rug.

⟨∞⟩

Less than an hour after Johnny had left, the sound of a crying baby woke Mary Anne. She looked around and found nothing, so she followed the cries to the house's main entrance. Upon opening the door, she saw a baby wrapped in a black cloak. He was in a basket. She picked him up, brought him in the house, and examined him.

"Aren't you a handsome little devil?" she said. "And with such beautiful skin, like porcelain." Mary Anne smiled as she observed a scar next to his eye. She rubbed it with the tips of her fingers. The baby stopped crying. At that, she beamed. After sitting down in a rocking chair while holding the stunning baby, Mary Anne exposed her breast, gently grabbed the back of the infant's head, pressed him against her bosom, and nursed him as only a monster could.

PART VII

The Devil's Truth

35

You know, you can't talk to some folks about nothing. They get right mad when you tell them what they don't want to hear. 'Cause they stuck in they ways. That's how some of them church folks is. I don't want you to think I'm badmouthing the Lord. I'm talking about the ones who sit in the pews. The people that act like they know everything. They think all the answers are in the Good Book. If everything is in the Bible, ain't no point in learning nothing else. That don't make sense now, do it? You think the Lord made the sun for you not to learn about it. What about the moon? And what about them great big ol' oceans that got His creations swimming deep?

You got to study other stuff to feed your soul. If you let it starve, it'll eat just about anything. A starving soul will turn you into one of them people that can look dead at an elephant and see a jackrabbit. You can't be that way. You got to believe them eyes the Lord gave you. If you act like it's a jackrabbit and not the elephant it is, you'll get yourself hurt. 'Cause when you go up to it and try to feed it a carrot, you'll get trampled to death. And you won't have nobody but yourself to blame. You can't lie to yourself about what you see. A person's lie is the devil's truth.

36

The day after Barkley and Galaxy made love would be just as spiritual, only they would leave the confines of their house on Church Street to go farther down the road to Liberty Baptist for a Sunday worship service filled with those who passed judgment. No one had predicted Barkley would show up, nor did they expect him to bring the little rich boy whose great-grandfather founded the whole town.

Although it was a slow progression to this moment, the love they made finalized their decision to let everyone know about their relationship. Not a single one of the many conversations they'd had could persuade Barkley, but the way he dominated Galaxy the previous night helped get him to that place. What better way to reveal themselves to the masses? Going to the barbershop was one thing, but crossing the threshold of Liberty Baptist Church was bold in a way that was foreign to Barkley. Thus, it was intrepid in a manner that unnerved poor Galaxy, who, though wanting to please his boyfriend, had deep reservations about going to that historic building just down the way.

The thought of parishioners worshipping a God he had never witnessed instilled uneasiness in Galaxy's psyche. The last time he stepped foot in a church was at his father's funeral. He remembered his mother's stoic expression, which contrasted with her usual nature. Galaxy respected the way she had carried herself, dressed in a black skirt and blazer. Dealing with death was one of the few times she stayed sober.

But now, Galaxy had other concerns. How would the members of Liberty Baptist Church take to him? Did they know what he and his boyfriend did last night? All he wanted from them was approval and acceptance. Coming to the realization that everyone had figured out what was going on between him and Barkley, Galaxy wished for the wherewithal to teach them about their romance so the people of Mansaville couldn't deny the intimate love one man could have for another.

"You ready, little man?" Barkley asked.

"Not yet," Galaxy responded as he tucked his shirt into his britches. "How do I look?"

"You look good." Words spoken with a proud smile.

Barkley had made sure Galaxy would be the best-dressed man at Liberty Baptist. He had bought his boyfriend a khaki suit and a pair of light-brown leather shoes. He himself wore a plain gray suit, a white shirt, and black shoes.

The couple left the house and migrated toward Liberty Baptist. Galaxy perspired as he slowed his stride. Barkley matched his pace and put his right arm around Galaxy's shoulder and let his boyfriend's arm wrap around his waist. As they marched toward the church, they would eventually join hands. But the display of affection wouldn't last long. Maybe they let go of each other because they were approaching hallowed ground, or perhaps the mere sight of people intimidated away the interlocking of their fingers. In a town that rained blood, people thought that two men holding hands was strange.

As they journeyed down Church Street, Barkley Jenkins Jr. reminisced about his grandmother and how she would cook for him and his father on Sundays. Yams, poke salad, mashed potatoes, fried okra, chitlins. And she would serve the meal with sweet tea that she always mixed with sliced oranges (the recipe you witnessed Barkley make in the kitchen weeks ago).

For nearly all his life, Barkley had resented going to church, considering it a time-consuming farce. His grandmother used to drag him to Liberty Baptist when he was a child, but, in her words, she would "turn it over to the Lord" and let her grandson find his own way. She held the firm belief that God and life experience delivered spirituality, not imperfect people. Sarah Jenkins felt that forcing Christianity on Barkley would have caused him to reject it even more, sending him down a path of unrighteousness. The last thing she wanted was to be absent of Barkley in the afterlife.

Now, as he and Galaxy advanced, Barkley looked up and thought of Grandma Sarah and how she had rescued him time and time again. Thinking of her revealed God to him. At this awakening, he put his arm around Galaxy and escorted him to Liberty Baptist.

Galaxy felt his heart pounding in his chest as he peered at the church sitting on a hill. In an effort to calm his nerves, he looked away and stared at the grass bordering the unpaved driveway as he and Barkley made the pilgrimage. He had never seen so many faces. They huddled in front of the church smiling at one another and saying, "Bless you." The men were suited up. As if to mock the heat, some women wore gloves boasting lace-lined wrists. The girls donned dresses that were red and yellow and blue and green and orange. The boys sported short-sleeved dress shirts, suspenders, and shorts, all running around with freezer pops they had stolen from the icebox in the church basement.

"Look at 'em, girl," a woman said. "I can't believe my eyes."

Not since the reverend and the deacon quelled rumors ten years ago had the congregation been so intrigued by a relationship. But Liberty Baptist Church had a way of indoctrinating them into obliviousness. They dismissed the grapevine banter about Johnny and Ray as fodder. And with a whispered truth sounding like a screaming lie to the willfully ignorant, the congregants stood steadfast behind their clergymen. How could the good reverend abuse himself with mankind and preach in the pulpit the next day? They chalked the rumors up to misunderstanding, and every Sunday they religiously paid for his Italian suits, his two sedans, and, ultimately, his second-biggest secret of all: the groundbreaking of the Tudor-style home he was building on the other side of the haunted river.

Unlike the grand home being constructed over there, Liberty Baptist Church stood humbly. There was no lobby to this church. Crossing the threshold led you straight to the main room, which was filled with rows of oak pews that ran from the front door and stopped within arm's reach of the pulpit. The carpet was a warm shade of green appearing to be an extension of the wild grass outside. It covered the entire floor, sprawling underneath the pews (the seats of which were padded with a velvety fabric of the same pasture-like green). The carpet also made its way to the stairs leading up to the reverend's lectern, which itself seemed a powerful structure. Aside from the large wooden cross hanging on the wall behind it, the lectern took center stage. Draped across it was a burnt-orange piece of fabric bearing a cross and boasting gold tassels that dangled just above the floor. Stained glass windows obstructed the natural light coming into the room. The walls were eggshell white. It was a chore for that lackluster color to march up the vaulted ceiling only to stop at the angle just underneath the steeple, but it made it there, just as Barkley and Galaxy had made it there, though they treaded with uncertain steps.

The hot air crashed into Galaxy's face as he ventured into Liberty Baptist Church, and the cool air soothed Barkley's countenance as he entered the holy temple for the first time in years. There was a mixture of colognes, perfumes, hair products, and old wood. The combination created a heavy scent, which Galaxy took in with every breath. Those who were already inside turned around and watched the couple poke along the aisle. No one could recall the last time a Goodfellow had entered the church for a Sunday worship service. When Galaxy and Barkley spotted an empty space in the third pew, Barkley stood in the aisle and motioned for his boyfriend to sit before he himself took the seat on the end.

"God bless you, young man. I'm Mrs. Hogan." She grabbed Galaxy's hand briefly as she spoke. "It's so nice of you to join us."

"Thank you. It's good to be here," Galaxy replied.

Mrs. Hogan's cordiality offered him a welcoming breeze like the one coming from the paper fan she waved below her chin.

"You look nervous. But don't you worry, baby. This is the Lord's house. There's no need to be nervous in here." She eyed his empty hands. "Do you have a copy of the Word?"

"No, ma'am."

"It's okay, baby. You can look on with me."

"Okay," Galaxy said.

"They usually have Bibles stuck in these little slots right here, but you know how folks steal . . . even in the church." Her smile brought more cool air to his face as Barkley sat quietly, looking toward the pulpit.

The people sitting in the pew just in front of them pressed their backs to their seats to get their ears as close to Galaxy and Mrs. Hogan's words as possible. That was the most anyone would attempt. They wised up and stopped staring at Galaxy (the few who did quickly cut their eyes when they thought he was looking at them).

"How are you, girl?"

"I'm doing fine, Mrs. Whitaker. How are you?" said a woman standing near the door.

"Just lovely." Mary Anne spoke in a light voice, as if trying to mimic an angel.

Overcoming the seeming impossibility of hearing Mary Anne's name in the crowd, Galaxy turned around and watched her. She stood there dressed in a pearl-colored suit and a Paris green blouse. Her makeup was a work of art: crimson lipstick, foundation in need of no blush, and a hint of bronze eye shadow. Mary Anne knew she was clean. There was no doubt she was the first lady of Liberty Baptist Church.

Galaxy's heart raced as he observed her. With her coat draped over her shoulders, Mary Anne escorted herself to the first pew, sat down, and picked up one of the flimsy fans. She rolled her eyes at Deacon Ray Jones, who was perched in a large chair behind the pulpit. When Ray caught sight of Galaxy, he bit his bottom lip. The deacon knew trouble was coming. All he could do was look back at the wooden crucifix on the wall and pray for a short service. Ray was always guarded when dealing with Mary Anne, and Galaxy's presence increased his defenses. He knew she wouldn't take kindly to the visitor. Though the deacon rarely talked to her one-on-one, he knew her well, based on conversations he and Johnny had about her. Ray realized the oddity in his lack of firsthand knowledge of this woman, his longtime neighbor and his wife's close friend and confidant. The deacon knew why he rarely spoke to Mary Anne, and she knew it, too.

The reason was her husband, Reverend Whitaker, who was entering the church, stopping to shake hands and pat his parishioners on their shoulders. He usually came in wearing his black robe over his suit, but not today. After kissing his wife on the cheek and nodding at the deacon, he sauntered to the lectern and spoke into the microphone as he pulled a white handkerchief from his coat pocket.

"Morning." He wiped his forehead with the cloth. "I said good morning."

"Good morning," the congregation responded, except Mrs. Whitaker.

"Just trying to see if you're awake. I don't know about y'all, but I'm feeling blessed today. Not because I got a new car or a fancy watch. Y'all know I ain't got none of those things." The crowd laughed. "But I'm blessed because I woke up this morning."

"Hallelujah."

"Preach it."

"We're going to start this service with a prayer. If it don't start right, it won't end right. Amen?"

"Amen."

"Would everyone please stand?"

Members of the congregation bolted upright and, except for Galaxy, bowed their heads.

The reverend said, "Let us pray." He wiped his forehead again. "Dear Lord, we thank you for this day. We thank you for the time to fellowship and praise your name. Lord, we know times can be rough, but with you by our side, we can overcome anything."

"Uh umm."

"Well."

"Dear Lord, we ask that you bless those in attendance today and those who wanted to be here but could not. And Lord, I ask that you even bless those who don't ever come. Help them find Jesus like I've found Jesus. And bless this church as we worship on this Sabbath day. In Jesus's name we pray. Amen."

"Amen," the congregation repeated as they sat down.

Galaxy had paid little attention to the reverend's prayerful words. His eyes had traveled back and forth between his own trembling hands and Mary Anne. The proximity to Mrs. Whitaker made his flesh crawl the way it did when he encountered her the first day he moved to this side of town. It had taken him weeks to realize she was the same woman who always sat on the porch in the house across the street. With that awareness, he would peek out of the front window before leaving the house in hopes she wasn't there.

"Well, we're going to have a good time in here today. There will be some shouting, some dancing, and some singing from the choir." The reverend looked out at the new attendee in the audience. "But first, we have to hear from any visitors." He gazed around as if talking to more than just Barkley's companion. Aside from those at the barbershop and a select few, no one had ever heard Galaxy's voice. Johnny, unlike his wife and the deacon, loved the presence of Galaxy in his church. The reverend envied and respected this young man's bravery.

He zeroed in on Galaxy's face. "If there are any new people here today, please stand and introduce yourself."

The crowd stared at Galaxy as his hands sweltered.

"It's all right, baby. Just get up and say a little something," said Mrs. Hogan, who held Galaxy's arm and stood up with him.

"He's a little bit nervous, but I told him he's in the Lord's house. So, he'll be just fine." She squeezed his wrist. "Go ahead, baby."

"Hi, everyone. My name is Galaxy Goodfellow. Don't let my last name scare you into liking me."

Everyone laughed, except the woman in the Paris green blouse.

"I've heard so many great things about worship services here at Liberty Baptist, and I'm glad to have the opportunity to experience it in person. I'm sure it will live up to its stellar reputation, especially since you have the best preacher in the South."

"That's right," an elderly man yelled.

"Sho' nuff."

"Thank you all so much for having me," Galaxy said.

"He did just fine, didn't he?" Mrs. Hogan asked. "I forgot to tell him we don't bite."

The parishioners laughed and applauded.

"Thank you, Mrs. Hogan," Galaxy said as he sat down.

She nodded her head and smiled while taking her seat.

"Good job, little man." Barkley wanted to kiss him on the cheek and hold his hand.

"Lordy Lordy," the reverend began, "it's always good to have new people come to the church and pay us a visit. Now, Galaxy, don't make this a one-time thing. Everyone is welcome here. The more people come, the more prayers we can send up to Jesus."

"Amen."

"All right now."

"I know that's right."

All of Galaxy's fears of rejection disappeared with the reverend's acknowledgment. But the feeling of acceptance would soon expire because Mary Anne boiled with rage, as borne out in the look on her face—the one in which her eyebrows almost met at the center of her forehead. When Johnny asked everyone to open their Bibles to read a passage, his wife defied the request.

She wanted to smear shit all over his microphone. Instead, she snatched her purse, sprang up, and stampeded toward the exit. Every man and woman in the church understood why. Even many of the children knew the reason. Some, particularly members of the choir who despised Mary Anne's constant criticism, were glad to see her go. By calling on Galaxy, the reverend had awoken the elephant to which Mary Anne had spent decades trying to feed a carrot, and no one could ignore the sound of her ego getting trampled.

With kidnapped dignity, Reverend Whitaker stuttered through his next line. Barkley frowned, Deacon Jones sat expressionless, and Betty Mae just shook her head. For his part, Galaxy Goodfellow sat in the miry clay. As she had before, Mary Anne turned a respectable affair into a trainwreck.

For it to be called organized religion, it certainly was messy and chaotic.

⌒ɯɯ৩

Though you have come to know Galaxy and Barkley well, they will disappear from this story for a while. You listened in on their conversations and followed them on their journey, so you may have gotten attached to them. But don't worry. They'll return soon enough. For now, the residents of Mansaville (including Old Scratch) would encourage you to take a break because this tale is about to take a rather strange turn.

Regardless of who you are, kudos for embarking on this quest. If you're a woman reading this, you get a pass. However, if you're a man who has made it this far, you may not be gay, but (at the very least) you've masturbated to gay porn. And that is quite all right. Notwithstanding your proclivities, enjoy the rest of the day, provided the solar rays still gleam. If, however, the sun has long set and the moon is visible in the dark sky, have a good night, dear reader . . . and the sweetest of dreams.

daggercide [dag-er-sīd]
noun
1. The killing or murder of a human being with a sharp object
Adjective form: daggercidal
Coined by Jermain L. Reeves
First recorded use: this novel

PART VIII
The Prince of Darkness

37

I 'member making dinner one Sunday for my son and grandson. It was just the three of us, but I cooked up a whole lot of food. You woulda thought an army was coming to town. I ain't never messed up a meal in my life, but Lord that turkey was terrible. We was all right, though, 'cause I just whipped up a little fried chicken instead. But I lost sleep trying to understand why I couldn't get that turkey right. And I finally figured out why. The outside was fresh as day, but the inside had done spoiled. See, the white lady that sold it to me didn't tell me about the rot. That's why she hurried up and took the money and shot off in the woods. I shoulda known something wasn't right 'cause I bought it over in Sugarlake where them white folks stay.

But it taught me a lesson about life. That turkey musta died from holding in too much bad stuff, the same way people hold in secrets. Ain't nothing worse than being spoiled around your heart. That inside spoil will kill you, so you gotta get it out by letting them secrets go. Even a good secret will turn into a lie. And them lies is what hurt you the most. Trying to 'member what you said and when you said it is a job by itself. So, you gotta retire from it. Retire to the truth so your heart will be clean. You don't want your last breath to be a secret the devil keeps.

They say the worst way to die is alone. But the truth is, the worst way to die is to rot from the inside out.

38

Johnny and Ray grew up before Liberty Baptist Church had blossomed into the historic institution it was when Galaxy had arrived. Johnny could recall when cloudy days forced them to use oil lamps to read from their hymn books because they lacked the money to pay for electricity. Back then, Liberty Baptist Church was a simple, white wooden building with a crooked steeple. Members of the congregation had to use the outhouse behind the church. Its grounds were bereft of a sign out front, and the winding driveway was a lawn of wildflowers and grass that was knee high to the toddlers who ran through it while attempting to avoid snake bites and ticks. Inside the church were no fancy oak pews, just chairs donated by residents who had a little something to spare.

The church was built prior to the civil rights movement, before Vietnam, even before the Second World War. When Johnny and Ray were children, principles came from parents, religion, history, and life. Before they were active members of the clergy, the two guys had each other, and that was their sole desire. When they were outside their homes and away from their parents, they were together. Their connection was so strong they even favored one another, and some mistook them as siblings. Johnny and Ray had the same dark brown faces, the same blackness at the knuckles, and the same deep eyes. When strangers asked them if they were brothers, Johnny and Ray would say "yes" in unison before giggling and dashing off to play. As age set in, their faces would lose their likeness, but as children, they were almost identical. And even more so, they were identically queer. They felt it even though they couldn't name it.

Thinking their kids were in need of siblings, the boys' parents assumed Johnny and Ray's relationship was a close brotherly bond between one only child and another. It would prove to be the biggest misjudgment they had about their offspring, neither of whom would ever give them the grandchildren they wanted.

No one inquired about their choice to share a sleeping bag when camping in the backyard, nor did anyone wonder why they dressed alike on the first day of school. Not a single person's eyebrows were raised when they exchanged intimate birthday presents once they were old enough to make money doing odd jobs. Because gays were nonexistent in Mansaville (especially on this side of the Confederate River), no one asked. Not their parents. Not their neighbors. And for a while, Johnny and Ray didn't even question themselves, despite having dry humped each other in the bushes behind the schoolhouse.

Years later, Ray went off to study English at South Carolina State University, and Johnny went to divinity school. Before they parted ways, Johnny told Ray, "I want to prove to everyone that I'm a man of God. Black people don't challenge ministers." Johnny sought to be what society wanted him to be. Therefore, he never allowed his feminine actions to show, and the times when they would (like when he crossed his leg too far over the other or when he put a hand on his hip), he would quickly change his demeanor.

Putting on a Christian front, he figured, was the best way to hide his identity. To that end, Johnny excelled at the seminary. He learned the Bible from front to back and became the most well-informed biblical scholar in the county. Most, particularly those of his generation, empowered him with their silence and followed him without a second thought, believing the reverend's grace to be their key to Salvation. This led him to build a large, loyal following of dedicated elders who had more power than any faction on the industrial side of the river. But even before all of this happened, Johnny thought getting a wife would help him craft an image that would convince the masses to take him seriously.

When Johnny married Mary Anne, he was sure to get Ray's blessing. With tears and an intimate kiss, his best friend gave his approval. Not to be outdone, Ray followed suit a year later with his own nuptial sham. There was no bachelor party for Ray; instead, there was a rendezvous between a married man and a fiancé. That day set a pattern in motion that would ruin four lives and mislead an entire people. Reverend Whitaker and Deacon Jones perpetuated deception with each secret kept. Not wanting to bring children into this false world, the only good decision Ray made was to pull out during the cum stroke to avoid getting his wife pregnant. Betty Mae, however, desperately wanted kids, and at least twice a week she would give him a pint. The poor woman was unaware that he fucked her from behind so he wouldn't have to look at her face.

Although Johnny attempted to start a family, his efforts conflicted with evil's wicked plan. You may remember when Johnny and Mary Anne fooled around in the woods to conceive Old Scratch. You may also recall that Johnny's penis had turned into a serpent while they were having sex. Well, that was a trick because the snake wasn't Johnny's beast. The venom that impregnated his wife didn't bear his seed. It belonged to evil itself, so Reverend Johnny Whitaker wasn't the father of Old Scratch.

39

Now it was 1997, decades after Johnny had married Mary Anne and months after Galaxy Goodfellow had moved into the house across the street. Johnny was at home taking a shower. When the water turned cold, he decided it was finally time to commit suicide and take his chances with Judgment Day. Fire would be his choice of how to die, thinking that burning on Earth would exempt him from meeting the same fate in hell.

Wanting to give his wife something before his death, Johnny made love to her that night, and the sex almost changed her views about his identity. She welcomed the intimacy, although she suspected there was a motive. Even still, Mary Anne pretended those moments were real as she was falling asleep in his arms.

Once his wife was in a deep slumber, he quietly got up, put on his clothes, and left her for good. When Johnny opened the door to the house, two candle flies came in and flew to the lamplight in the living room. (Mary Anne insisted this light be left on when she was home alone.) One of the candle flies died by the lampshade that night. The other one flew back outside in solitude. Though the insect was free, it would never return to the home of lights it once knew.

There were also no comforting lights to guide Johnny at 1:00 a.m. on this Monday, seconds after he had shut the door, trapping one of the death-bound insects inside. He stashed a garbage bag in the trunk of his sedan. The contents of the sack clanged against the spare tire. Johnny lifted his head and looked around to see if anyone heard the noise, pleased that no one was around and even more content with the silence of the German shepherd in Betty Mae's backyard.

Johnny opened the car door and sat in the driver's seat. He put the key in the ignition and turned it enough for the dashboard indicators to come on. He rolled down the windows and drummed up enough courage to crank the car, listening for the barking dog and looking for passersby. He backed the car out of the driveway and headed to Liberty Baptist Church.

The moonlight shone as best it could through the thick clouds scattered about the sky. The few visible stars were the only pleasant things this day would offer Mansaville. It was evident that rain was coming. The reverend wept as he parked his vehicle on the road in front of the church. After getting out of the car and removing the black bag from the trunk, Johnny ambled the winding gravel road leading to the front door of the holy temple. The contents of the bag, though light, weighed him down and turned an ordinary stroll into a difficult journey.

Upon reaching the church, he trudged up the few stairs leading to the heavy doors. When going to church alone, he typically would step around back to use the side entrance. But this time, the reverend expected no encounters, save for the one with his conscience.

"Lord, forgive me, for I am about to sin," he spoke, opening the door and crossing the threshold of Liberty Baptist Church.

He traipsed down the carpeted aisle toward the altar, ignoring everything in the room except the pulpit he had owned every Sabbath day for decades. When arriving at the altar, Johnny put the bag down and stood at the podium. Straining to look out at the empty pews, he adjusted the microphone and clutched each side of the lectern as if he were about to speak. But the minister couldn't say a word; all he could do was blink to keep from crying.

The brass collection plates, sitting in a stack on a small table, rested behind him. So did the chair in which Deacon Jones would sit and scream out *amens* and *preach it, brothers* to encourage his best friend. Johnny went to the table and placed his pocket change in the shiny plate on top of the stack. That would be the last time the reverend would tithe at Liberty Baptist Church.

He walked toward the black garbage bag, opened it, and removed a metal container of lighter fluid. He pried the bottle open and doused the flammable liquid on everything at the altar: the lectern, Ray's chair, his own chair, and even the bottom of the wooden cross that hung on the wall and towered over the church. Relieved that the cross lacked a sculpture of Jesus Christ, to the reverend it was just two perpendicular slats of oak with symbolism but no authority.

All of the good memories Johnny had at the church raced through his mind. He reminisced about the time he and Ray lost their virginity to each other out back behind Mister Tree, the oak where countless slaves were hanged. The reverend thought of his mother's funeral and how peaceful she looked in the rose casket, after having died of a spider-driven heart attack just a week after her husband and Johnny's father succumbed to lung cancer. He even recalled the few times he and his wife would laugh in the back office after church let out. The nostalgic ponderings prompted a sense of guilt that took control of Johnny, forcing him to do what he would normally do after having cheated on his wife. He offered a prayer:

"Lord, I have sinned. I know I'm an adulterous liar, but is sinning really a bad thing when it's justified? Answer me for once. I always talk to you, but you never speak. If you're there, come forward, and show your face. It's funny how you get to hide all day long, but when I hide, it's called lying. Why do I have to be the one to suffer? I am old and withering away, O Lord. Give me strength. Give me truth. Give me freedom. I've been trapped in this world, this town, that house, that marriage, this life. I know your Son is coming back one day. Send Him now with all the fire of hell and deliver me. I need deliverance. Deliverance from wrong.

"But it feels so natural. How is it wrong? Answer me! This isn't lust, Lord. It's the kind of love I would die for. Death? What is death? Is it when the heart stops beating, the lungs stop breathing, the blood stops flowing? Is that what death is?

"Well, then, I'm dead already. My heart stopped beating a long time ago 'cause I can't fully express the love that's in it. I stopped breathing years ago 'cause I'm so buried in lies I need air. As for blood? I've been crucified, too. I've been cut, beaten, cut, and beaten some more. I have no blood left to spill. So I guess that means I'm dead. I don't even want to resurrect. I want to go away forever. That's what I'm asking for."

When he finished his supplication, Johnny continued to kneel and clutch his hands. And like Mary Anne (mother of the devil) and Mary (mother of Jesus), Reverend Whitaker wept in the midst of an unanswered prayer, for Johnny realized he was the candle fly that would never return home.

40

Reverend Whitaker was still weeping, clutching his hands, and kneeling in prayer at the altar when a gust of wind collided with his neck. The candles flickered, swaying in unison as if engaging in a Sunday praise dance. But this was early Monday morning, and an unusually cold one. The candles lining the altar flamed out, except the one resting underneath the picture of Jesus. Its light cast a shadow on the wall in front of the reverend. It took the shape of a person's increasing silhouette with moving legs.

"This is a sign," the reverend whispered, still stooping on the floor, though his hands were no longer prayerful.

"Yes, it is," Old Scratch said in a low tenor as he advanced.

The reverend stood up and turned around. All he could see was a set of green eyes floating toward him, as the one working candle tried to fight off the darkness.

"Are you an angel?" Johnny asked.

"I was . . . once." The tenor changed to a baritone as the other candles rekindled, bringing more light—though it was ever so dim. Fog broke into the church and mobbed the green eyes that floated toward him.

"Who are you?" The reverend picked up a Bible and held it toward Old Scratch.

The thick haze disappeared to reveal the devil, whose eyes sparkled like emeralds in the moonlight. There Old Scratch was—naked with his hands behind his back. His lean muscles showed every line and curve of his body, accentuated by the unshaven pubic hair that reached toward his navel. As he grazed the grass-colored carpet, Old Scratch's long, thick penis swung back and forth, slowly tapping his thighs, which bore strands of hair that contrasted with his porcelain skin. He moved in regality. Like King Mansa Musa, he was royalty, for this man was Old Scratch, the Prince of Darkness.

Eyeing the smooth foreskin of Old Scratch's penis, the reverend put the Bible over his own crotch.

"An erection is a natural thing, my friend. There's no need to hide it," Old Scratch said.

"You've come to save me." Johnny let out a breath.

Old Scratch smiled as he stretched out one of his arms. The other was still behind his back, grasping a long knife.

The reverend approached him, fell to his knees, and placed the Bible on the floor. The Good Book sparked as it touched Old Scratch's left foot. The Prince of Darkness stepped back in pain that quickly dissipated. Still kneeling, the reverend moved toward him. He cried like a child as he wrapped his arms around Old Scratch's left thigh, hugging firmly. The reverend pressed the side of his face against the devil's penis, which felt warm and safe to the touch. The Prince of Darkness stroked Johnny's gray hair.

"Remove all of your clothes," Old Scratch said.

The reverend stood up and followed the orders while examining the devil's body in awe.

"You're beautiful," Johnny said.

"Yes, I know." The devil became a tenor again. "Embrace me, my friend."

Johnny did, as he rested his chin on Old Scratch's head. "I'm so glad you came to help me." Another tear fell from his face. "You're here to rescue me, right?"

"Something like that," Old Scratch said with a smirk. He then stabbed the reverend in the middle of the back, releasing a stream of blood.

"No." Johnny gasped as his frame went limp.

Before closing his eyes, he saw a vision of his mother and father shaking their heads. They were right to be disappointed in the son who was just murdered by the devil against whom he preached. Here in this church, the Prince of Darkness had committed the most significant daggercide in Mansaville's history, despite having taken countless lives in this very town. Old Scratch didn't care much for torturing people, but he loved killing them.

So, he smiled as the reverend's lifeless body banged against the floor. Another gust of wind blew through the church. It was the devil's breath of evil. The fire in one of the candles intensified with the wave of Old Scratch's hand. He made a similar motion to force the candle to fall, the flames hitting the lighter fluid with which the reverend had doused the church. The fire strengthened and performed its own evil praise dance as it took on the shape of bodies sitting in every burning pew.

The parishioners of fire sat and watched the devil wrap a rope around the neck of Johnny's dead, naked body. As the devil picked up the reverend's remains, the congregation of fire jumped up and waved their hands, rocking like trees in the hot wind. The flaming bodies howled in unison as blazes consumed the green carpet and barreled toward the altar and up the walls. The crucifix fell with a thud and found itself covered in flames. At that, Old Scratch smiled as he carried the body outside to Mister Tree.

Poor Johnny is what you might say while looking at the pierced corpse and the handle of the knife shining in the firelight of Liberty Baptist Church. The reverend never should have fallen prey to evil by living a lie that had become a decades-long sharp object in his back. Why did he accept a hug from the ruler of hell when he had the choice to go down a path of righteousness?

It's because he forgot the very thing you must remember: When the devil embraces you with one hand, you can never see the knife in the other.

PART IX
Maxine

41

Long 'fore she gave birth to Galaxy, Maxine had some kind of life. But it sho'nuff started to go downhill the day she slung hot grits on her husband, David. Lord, he liked to pass out when it scalded him. He ran out that big ol'mansion like a rat, his little legs steady moving. Thank God she didn't hit him upside the head. Just a little got on his arms, so he was all right after he put some castor oil on it. He should've used butter. Them rich folks don't know nothing. Anyhow, her husband, David, took it in his head to call her out her name. Maxine sat right quiet and went to the kitchen. He should've known something was up 'cause she ain't step foot in that kitchen but a handful of times to do some cooking. She opened the cabinet to get a box of them good Aunt Jemima grits and poured some in a pot she done already put some heat under. She was justa humming and stirring like there wasn't nothing wrong. Time the water came to a boil, she went to his study, where she knowed he was. He could smell the food 'fore she even got in the room. The crazy girl even put a little pepper in the grits like they was about to be put on a plate and served for dinner. But she slung them at him and got his shoulder and arm pretty good. She had a little left in the pot and tried to get at him again. She wusta waited by the door, but she ran to his desk. That gave him room to run, so he shot outta the house and didn't come back for two days. Spent the night at the whiskey factory. He never called her out her name again.

The problem is, women call themselves out they own names with the things they do. Putting on all this crazy makeup and straightening they hair like white women just to get a man. Girl, that ain't your pretty. That's them chemicals. They don't just eat at your scalp. They eat at your soul. Beauty can't be found in no box and no bottle. Them girls wonder why they so sad. You'll always be sad when you look in the mirror and see box perm beauty looking back at you. Men ain't got to do all that to look good. They roll out the bed, wipe the crust out they eyes, and that's it. That's why they ain't got as much pressure.

I had love in my own heart 'cause I held on to what the Lord gave me. Natural hair. Big thighs. Dark skin. That's why I was happy. 'Cause I was me—not magazine me but the real me. And I didn't do what Maxine did, chasing a man's money. When you do that, you setting yourself up. Money can't buy happiness, but running after it can get you sadness. Making money who you are and what your marriage is about can make it even worse. Y'all girls can have your fancy clothes and fake hair. If a man got that stuff for you 'cause you gave him your goods, you ain't nothing but a hooker. Anything that's bought can be thrown away. If your man bought you, one day he'll throw you away, too.

Poor Maxine. Her husband treated her that way 'cause he bought her from a thrift store. With that smart mind she had and all that talent, she could've been something, but she threw it away to marry a Goodfellow. You call it a come up. I call it hooking. Not all prostitutes stand on the corner.

42

Nineteen fifty-five was the year the Vietnam War started. It also marked the third year of President Dwight D. Eisenhower's first term. To Mansaville, however, it was the year a gang of white men lynched Leroy Walker after he bought soda from a store. In that same year, on August 7, Maxine Webster was born in the hospital in Mansaville. Her mother smiled when she realized she had given birth to a beautiful girl who already had a full head of hair. This was taken as a sign of looming precociousness. Maxine, so named because her father was expecting a boy whom he wanted to name Maxwell, came as a surprise, though neither parent was disappointed upon seeing that her skin was a radiant shade of dark brown they had never seen.

Maxine was the youngest of three. Having two older brothers forced her to toughen up and take on a competitive drive that wasn't in her nature. Her father, a manager at the whiskey factory, had made sure she had access to the finer things: music lessons, a tutor, and horseback riding. Her mother stayed home but occasionally worked as a seamstress, setting her money aside for her children's college fund to which Satchel Goodfellow added money every year. Once Maxine was placed in gifted classes and excelled as a pianist, Satchel identified her as the future wife of his grandson, David, and he would quietly pay for things to groom her into becoming a Goodfellow, even calling the president of Spelman College and funding a scholarship to cover her full tuition. He also provided a stipend, allowing her to live comfortably while other college students struggled.

The Order of Black Dragons had arranged a meeting between

David Goodfellow and Maxine. She thought it was a chance encounter, but the rendezvous was a successful ploy to plant the seed that would grow into a romance and ultimately a marriage with David. Her eventual distinction as the valedictorian of Spelman College would further deem her suitable for marrying someone from the Morehouse Machine, although it would be decades before the secret would be revealed to her. Despite her academic achievement and relocating to Washington, DC, to be with David while he attended Howard University College of Dentistry, she wasn't worthy of knowing about the blue fire that leveled the playing field. She too attended Howard University, earning a master's in French language and literature. That would be yet another reason for her to become a member of the family because every Goodfellow was expected to have at least a master's degree. As soon as Maxine enrolled in the graduate program, Satchel and his wife began planning the wedding that would take place in Mansaville. It would be the most illustrious ceremony anyone in town had ever seen.

Maxine herself had been impressed by her own wedding, which was held at Liberty Baptist Church. The color scheme, light blue and silver, went well with the flowers of which she herself was unaware until seeing them during her walk down the aisle in a dress someone else had picked for her. While being escorted by her ailing father, she realized her marriage would be an arrangement, not a union built on love. When her groom lifted the veil from her face, he saw tears running down his bride's countenance, a sign he interpreted as joy, though her tears were as thick and depressing as Confederate rain. But Maxine Webster still loved David. Beyond that, she thought she was *in* love with him, so "I do" seemed like the right words to utter. However, the kiss—the definitive consummation—confirmed how David had misconstrued her tears. The contact of their lips felt processed and manufactured, like some ingredient to a secret recipe a stranger had created.

The reception was held at the Goodfellow estate. As the festivities were underway downstairs, Maxine sat on the end of her bed in a shiny slip that, earlier in the evening, had been covered with a red strapless dress that had turned every head in the house. Despite her stepfather's discouragement, twenty-four-year-old Maxine wore the ensemble anyway in a poor attempt to look sexy. More so, it represented her efforts to reclaim her identity and freedom.

A collective gasp went through the mansion as she entered the living room. When she had gone upstairs to get dressed, the room was the usual array of antique furniture and impressionist art, but when she descended the spiral staircase, it was full of Mansaville's finest dignitaries, all of whom, especially her husband and father-in-law, were appalled at the scantily clad Maxine.

"Young girls wear anything these days." The guests all laughed. "She told us she would try to embarrass us." Turning to Maxine, "You silly little thing."

The elder Mrs. Goodfellow's wit eased the tension in the room, and no one thought much more about Maxine's short dress and fishnet stockings. Aside from occasional glances and chuckles at what they now perceived as a harmless prank, the elite group continued as normal with champagne in their grips. Servants moved about with silver trays balanced on one hand as they faked smiles at bad jokes. All the while, Satchel was incensed. No one rebelled against him, and whoever tried to do so would be punished dearly, especially if their defiance manifested itself in Mansaville, the mecca he had founded. Little did either of them know that Old Scratch had picked out Maxine's trashy outfit and laid it on the bed for her to see. He knew Maxine's vulnerability would impede her judgment, but he also recognized that Satchel, even in his old age, couldn't resist a woman in a red dress, even one who had just married his grandson.

Old Scratch, disguised as a servant, had convinced everyone but Satchel and Maxine to go for a walk. Satchel had never let white people in his home and would later confront the owner of the catering company, but he appreciated the opportunity Old Scratch had made available, though he was concerned about Old Scratch's handling of food. When visiting someone's home years ago, Satchel witnessed a white woman pet her dog and knead biscuits without having washed her hands. That was all it took for him to refrain from eating white people's cooking. Now, however, that was an issue he would deal with later, as he allowed the devil to entice him. Distracted by his libido, Satchel ignored the blue sparks in his own hands when he shook the right one of the devil himself. Satchel would later be able to remember where he had seen the devil's green eyes, but by then, it would be too late for him and for Maxine because he had made the mistake of drinking whiskey the devil had poured.

When the mansion was empty of guests and the hired help had been dismissed, Satchel went up to his granddaughter-in-law's room. When he opened the door, she sprung from her bed and covered herself with her towel. The dress she had worn, along with her black stockings, lay on the bed. The sight of those garments brought back the same anger that had filled him.

Old Scratch laughed. Satchel and Maxine couldn't hear or see him.

"You never should have drunk the whiskey I gave you, old man," the devil said to himself as he sat in the corner of the room.

It turns out, Old Scratch was right because the alcohol he had spiked with his own blood put a hex on the elderly Satchel, who for the first time in nearly a decade hadn't needed help getting up the stairs. Although the windows were closed, wind blew throughout the room. An evil melody sounded off—not the singsong of whip-o-wills, but the dark chant of skeletons lining up outside the house.

As if on cue, the whiskey took hold of Satchel's body something terrible. His posture firmed up. The remaining gray hairs on his head grew to become fuller before turning to shiny black. The wrinkles on his forehead disappeared, as did those on his face and eventually those on the rest of his body. He grunted when his dentures fell from his mouth, pushed out by pearly teeth growing from his gums. The shakes that had overtaken his hands over the years had vanished, leaving young, steady hands that he used to remove his shirt, revealing the same chest he had decades ago.

"What's happening?" Maxine asked in a calm, soft tone that attempted to mask her fear.

The hellish choir of skeletons sang louder as a now young and shirtless Satchel prowled, wearing a pair of gray trousers, black socks, and a pair of dress shoes that tapped rhythmically against the hardwood floors. He pulled his pants down to expose his genitals. Maxine Goodfellow cried at the sight of his erect penis.

"You want to embarrass the family by dressing like a slut?" His voice was still old.

"What are you doing, Mr. Goodfellow? Please go away!" Maxine pleaded.

He lurched and slapped her in the face. Red sparks flew from his hand, but having braced for a blow, his prey didn't notice. Satchel pushed Maxine. Her crying intensified as she found herself on her back, her towel having been ripped away.

"Stop!" Maxine held up her hands.

Red fire consumed them while he raped her, but with her eyes closed, Maxine missed the flames once again.

"Jesus, help me," she said.

At that, Old Scratch snickered. They still couldn't detect his sounds.

All Maxine could hear was Satchel's moans while feeling his sweat drip onto her grimacing face.

The fire disappeared.

Satchel grew old again. He struggled to get off of her. He tried his best to pull up his pants, succeeding after several attempts. Too feeble to pick up his dentures, Satchel was forced to stand there toothless. Old Scratch thought that was cute.

Maxine felt discarded and filthy as she lay there thunderstruck.

"If you tell anyone about this, there will be consequences," Satchel said in a tone as hot as fire.

"I understand." Her voice was as cold as ice.

She didn't understand, however, that a victim's silence is a predator's currency. Her decision to keep the rape a secret empowered Satchel. The people of Mansaville would remain unaware that he raped Maxine, and no one would know this act of sexual assault was how her son Galaxy was conceived.

43

That night, Maxine wore an elegant black dress that draped down her body and spread out at the floor. She was careful to have put on a shiny slip to cover what was stolen. She sat down at her vanity and made up her face: foundation, a touch of burgundy blush, and flesh-colored lipstick softened with the press of her lips to a napkin.

Gently stroking her long, dark tresses with a wooden brush, she rubbed her free hand across her hair, following the tracks of the brush-strokes. Before standing, Maxine sprayed a little perfume on that part of the neck just under the chin.

The best addition: a stunning, if not dazzling, pair of slingbacks.

While strutting down the hallway, she smiled thinking about the times her father would take her outside of her childhood home and push her on the homemade swing as the wind carried her giggles all the way to the ocean.

Maxine descended the staircase and stood in the foyer. She went outside and ran across the front lawn, holding her evening gown at the thighs. It was cold out, but her slip kept her warm despite the thinness of the fabric out of which her gown was made. "David would love the way I look now," she said to herself just before running to an old swing that used to hang from a thick branch on the evergreen. The swing had been torn down the previous fall when a Confederate rain-storm came through and detached the wooden board.

Despite what had just happened to her, Maxine took solace in knowing she was a Goodfellow with newfound access to wealth. Why had she stared at a container of alcohol while her in-law was about to rape her? Green eyes, nestled in the bottle's glass, had gazed at her. Underneath the emerald organs of sight, lips moved, telling her to drink. As the devil's eyes blinked, his tears dripped into the whiskey, giving it the sweet taste of temptation. Now, as Maxine sat down on a stone bench overlooking a pond, those same eyes (seemingly suspended in the air) floated toward her, causing her heart to race.

"Who are you?" she asked.

Just as she posed the question, the green eyes stopped floating, and she could see the person to whom they belonged. She recognized him as an employee of the catering company.

"You startled me," Maxine said.

"I'm sorry, sweetheart. That was not my intention," Old Scratch responded, still wearing the work uniform bearing the logo of an angel.

"It's okay now that I know you're not a monster."

"Well, not exactly." Old Scratch smiled, his eyes the color of American money.

"What does that mean?" Maxine laughed.

"Nothing, sweetheart. I just came to check on you."

"Why? Do I look distressed?" Maxine asked.

"Why, no. But it has been my experience that there is a problem when a well-dressed woman is sitting outside alone."

"You're very observant." Maxine noticed his eyes resembled those that had reflected in the bottle.

"Here, Mrs. Goodfellow." He handed her a container of whiskey and said, "This may ease the pain. I find it always helps me in my time of need."

"I'm not much of a drinker, but thank you," Maxine said as she looked at the bottle, a product of the family into which she had just married. "Well, why not?"

"Yes, why not? No one else is here."

"Of course no one else is around. My husband is already off doing business. He can't take a break, not even for us to have a proper honeymoon."

"This can be your honeymoon." He pointed at the alcohol.

"Well, there you have it." She looked at his hands. "Do you have a glass?"

"Sorry, no."

"A Goodfellow woman would never drink directly from the bottle," Maxine said.

"When you're feeling down, what does it matter?"

"Good point." Maxine opened the container and took a sip, surprised by its sweetness.

"Not what you expected?" Old Scratch asked.

"No, not at all."

"Keep drinking."

"You don't have to tell me twice." She laughed.

"I finally got you to smile."

"It's the whiskey, honey. Don't flatter yourself." She moved her hand as if flicking crumbs from a table.

The devil chuckled as Maxine drank.

"I'll leave you to yourself."

"Wait. I never got your name," Maxine said, still savoring the saccharine beverage.

"It doesn't matter. No one knows my real name anyway." He smirked and spirited away, taking his money-colored eyes with him.

She turned the bottom of the bottle toward the moon and finished off the whiskey. A rich man's wife sat all alone on the night of her wedding. Maxine Goodfellow had reached her dream, but she was still a sad girl because her love was bought, not built. It would've done her some good to have met an older, wiser woman. Grandma Sarah would've warned her about being one of those women who sell themselves for the so-called good life. After taking in this advice, Maxine would've understood that she herself was nothing but a prostitute.

And she was a cheap one at that. Her pussy belonged on the clearance rack.

44

At 1:00 p.m. on a Saturday, just after having finished lunch, Galaxy went to the bedroom to change the linens. The Tiffany Blue and brown color scheme had taken its course, so he opted for an all-white arrangement resembling one of the guest bedrooms of his childhood home. As he stood on his toes reaching for the comforter, he heard a car pull into the driveway.

He crept to the window, bent one of the blinds down, and almost fainted at the sight of his mother, a woman to whom he had not spoken in months. Surprised she had abandoned box-perm beauty to embrace her natural hair, Galaxy smiled, having never seen her look so liberated. Sporting dreads and wearing a simple white blouse tucked into a pair of dark blue jeans, Maxine had just gotten out of the Lincoln Town Car in which she had been chauffeured. Her black open-toed shoes matched the pocketbook she toted. Sapphire earrings dangled from her ears. Although it was July, she had the moodiness of the month of April, unsure of whether to be hot or cold.

"I shouldn't be long," Maxine said to the driver as she stood on Barkley and Galaxy's porch. After feeling a cool breeze hit her back, she hugged herself and turned around, "Where did that come from?" she whispered to herself while eyeing the Whitaker residence across the street.

Maxine surveyed the home where her son lived. After observing the gray paint peeling from the porch, she shook her head, fished a handkerchief from her purse, and wrapped it around the index finger she used to ring the doorbell.

By now, Galaxy was already on the other side of the door. He took a breath, exhaled, and opened it.

"My son."

"Hi, Mother." Galaxy wanted to reach out for a hug but put his arms by his sides like a soldier at attention, or more aptly, one not at ease.

"Your hair," Galaxy said.

"Yes, dear. It was time for a change. Freedom is a special thing." Maxine raised her eyebrows. "This is the part where you're supposed to invite me in."

Galaxy opened the door wider. Maxine crossed the threshold into a house she looked down on, although it was similar to the one in which she grew up.

They looked at each other and embraced. Now her mood matched the warmth of July, except her tears showered like April rain.

"I missed you, Galaxy." She offered a smile.

"Have a seat." He kept his smile to himself.

"Okay."

"How did you know I was here?" Galaxy asked.

"I'm a Goodfellow, and so are you. We can't possibly hide for long in this town."

"The story of my life," Galaxy said.

"Plus, word gets around." She crossed her right leg over her left and added, "But I must say, it didn't travel as fast as I thought it would."

"You didn't try to contact me."

"Why? My sources told me you were safe. Besides, the way you left suggested you didn't want to be contacted."

"That's fair," Galaxy said with a nod.

"You were embarrassed, I know."

"Yes, I was."

"I already knew, Galaxy. I've known since you were a toddler."

"Really?" He turned toward her and leaned forward.

"Mothers know these things," Maxine said with a grin, her red lipstick glistening.

"Can I get you something to . . ."

"No. Just listen. Don't try to change the subject," Maxine said, raising her hand, not her voice.

"Okay."

She gazed forward. "Son, I've never had a problem with gay people. It would be hypocritical of me."

"What?" Galaxy asked, his eyebrows attempting to reach his hairline.

"I had a little fun with girls in my day." She gave him a side eye, accompanied with a smirk.

"That's disgusting, Momma."

"Not as disgusting as what I witnessed you doing with that white man."

"You had to go there, didn't you?" Galaxy rolled his eyes.

They laughed.

Putting his hand on his chest, Galaxy said, "So, you're . . ."

"No, lesbianism is not for me. It was fun, but that's about it. Men interest me most, emotionally and physically, especially physically," Maxine said.

"That's enough." He managed to frown and smile at the same time.

"You're an adult now, Galaxy. You should be able to have an adult conversation."

"Not about this."

"I get it," she said.

"But I do have something to ask you," Galaxy said.

"Then ask."

"If you didn't have a problem with me being . . . uh—"

"Gay," Maxine interrupted.

"Yes, gay."

"Go on."

"If you didn't have a problem with it, why did you always treat me the way you did?" Galaxy asked.

"What do you mean? Putting you in the best schools? Making sure you were fed?"

"Stop it. You know what I'm talking about."

"Enlighten me, Galaxy."

"The constant criticism, acting like I wasn't good enough, always snapping at me as if you were annoyed with everything I did."

"I was scared." She looked away from him.

"Of what?"

"Your fire," she replied.

"You know? How?" Galaxy asked.

"I raised you, remember." She peered at the wall. "It would come out of your little hands when you were a wee thing. You even had a ball of fire in your hand the day you were born. I chalked it up to my being tired from giving birth. I tried to put it out of my mind until I brought you home. I burped you and put you in the crib with your rattle. Your tiny hands could barely clutch it. You reached for it, and a spark came out of your fingers. I jumped back and screamed and ran out of the room."

"You were scared of me?" Galaxy asked, though offering a declarative tone.

"Yes, afraid of my own child. Can you even comprehend what that does to a mother?"

"No, I can't," Galaxy answered, barely allowing her to finish the question.

"I understand. But just imagine how terrifying it was. It doesn't scare you, Galaxy, because it's all you know."

"So, why aren't you afraid of me now?" Galaxy asked.

"Because your dad told me about an underground organization just before he died. He said he was breaking a sacred pact by telling me but that I needed to know." Maxine unfolded her arms and looked at the television, though it was turned off. "We argued about you so much, Galaxy. He would say I was crazy and just imagining it, and it put a wedge between us. I knew what I was seeing. And I . . ."

"Took it out on me," Galaxy said, not grasping the importance of her mentioning the secret society.

"Yes."

"Even though you were scared of me? That doesn't make sense," he said.

"It doesn't make sense to me, either, Galaxy, but I'm trying here . . . I'm trying to explain."

"Go on," Galaxy whispered.

"I thought you were some kind of demon, but as the years went by, you never hurt me. You never hurt anyone. Not even the guys who bullied you in school. I realized the powers you had were benign. But I was still horrified."

"I'm sorry for being the way I am." Galaxy cried in front of her for the first time since he was a baby.

"No. Don't be sorry. It's a gift. I now know what it is. Although I understand why your father kept it a secret, it would've helped our marriage if he had told me sooner. He kept quiet about your powers because that's what he was told to do."

"Told by whom? And did he have any powers?" Galaxy asked without pausing between the two questions.

Ignoring the first one, she replied, "I don't know. I don't think so. It must have skipped over him and gone to you."

"Maybe so." Galaxy, too, looked at the blank television screen.

"Well, I guess I should get going."

"Not yet, Momma." Galaxy put his hand on her shoulder. "There's something I want you to explain."

"What's that, dear?"

"The constant drinking."

"Oh, yes, that," Maxine said as she leaned forward on the couch.

"Was that because of me?"

"Heavens no. Not in the least."

"Then why?" Galaxy asked.

Maxine thought of the time she had been raped. A tear rolled down her face.

"What's wrong, Momma?"

"Everything. But that's a conversation for a different day."

"Okay," Galaxy replied.

"I almost forgot. I have one more thing to tell you."

"Yes?" Galaxy asked.

"You're going back to Morehouse."

"Yes, I'm returning for the fall semester," Galaxy said.

"That wasn't a question."

"I understand." He looked at the floor.

"You've only missed one semester, so you can easily make that up."

"I will."

"I know you will. You'll be a Morehouse graduate in a couple of years, and I can't wait to see you walk across that stage," she said.

"I'll make you proud."

"I'm already proud of you." Maxine didn't realize she was twirling one of her dreads. "I just want to make sure you get the education you deserve, but you have to work hard."

"I know. That's what Goodfellows do."

"That's right." Maxine beamed. "I'm glad I raised you here in Mansaville."

"Why?"

"You got to see a city run and owned by black people. And everything was just fine, wasn't it?"

As if the town had not been haunted, Galaxy replied, "Better than fine."

"Yes, it is, and you know it kills white folks to see our success. But it means they'll come after us one day. There'll be a war, Galaxy. There always is."

"And they're always the aggressor," Galaxy said.

"I'm wasting my breath since you already know."

The sky rumbled.

"The Confederate storm is coming. I better get going," Maxine said.

"You never get used to their blood, do you?"

"Never." She stood up and made her way to the window. "The sky is getting red, so it won't be long. I have to get across the river."

"Okay." Galaxy bolted up and followed her.

"Another thing."

"Yes, ma'am?"

"That house across the street." She pointed in the direction of Mary Anne's home. "You need to stay away from there. There's bad energy coming out of it. So, be careful, dear. I don't know who or what lives there, but something isn't right."

"I understand," Galaxy said while looking out the window at Mary Anne's house as if he had never seen it. He wondered how his mother could know such a thing.

Maxine grabbed his hand and said, "I want you to come home to see us before you go back to college. Your sister misses you."

"I miss her, too. Tell her I love her."

"I will." She let go of his hand.

"It'll do her some good. She's been so depressed since your father died."

"I've been depressed, too."

"So have I, but at least I got control of the money now," Maxine said with a grin.

"Momma, stop it," Galaxy said, his words competing with a chuckle.

"Too soon?"

"Way too soon."

"I got everything except the money he left in a trust for you. Soon you'll have the details." She coiled another one of her locks. "Once you're back at the dorm, I'll send your banking information and the terms of the trust, but it pales in comparison to the one the Order of Black Dragons has."

"The Order of Black Dragons? What's that?"

"In due time." She put a hand on each of his shoulders. "Just know you're not alone."

"I want to know what all of this means." Galaxy's voice soared to the ceiling. "You can't drop a name like the Order of Black Dragons and not explain it. The name alone sounds crazy."

"I'll tell you in the near future. Be patient, girl."

"Girl?" Galaxy asked with a smile. "We're not there yet, Momma."

Their laughter filled the room.

The Confederate thunder roared like a cub, forcing Galaxy to put his inquiry on hold.

"Well, that's my cue. You know to stay indoors," Maxine said.

"I know that, Momma. Everyone in Mansaville knows."

"Okay," Maxine said as she hugged him. "I love you, son, and I'm sorry for all I've done."

"I love you, too, Momma. You don't need to apologize. I understand now."

"Thank you for that." Maxine relaxed the embrace.

They both understood more work needed to be done to repair their relationship, but they were satisfied, knowing this was a start. Galaxy opened the door. She crossed the threshold. Confederate thunder roared, this time like an adult lion.

"I better go." Maxine scampered to the car.

Galaxy then saw his mother do something he had never known her do. She waved off the driver and opened the car door herself. What he wouldn't see were the tears falling from her eyes as she mused over going back to tell him Satchel was his real father. Maxine settled on withholding this from him, the same way Mary Anne's mother stayed quiet, having passed away with the identical secret neatly stashed away in the tobacco tin where bad memories are kept. Like Galaxy, Mary Anne was the product of rape. And Satchel Goodfellow was the rapist, making Galaxy and Mary Anne brother and sister.

As you take a moment to process this revelation, remember being told in the second chapter that this would be a family saga. Now you understand why. As you also know, Mary Anne gave birth to the demon baby named Old Scratch. Therefore, Galaxy is the devil's uncle. This means that (in the early stages of this tale) Galaxy was fucked up the ass by his own nephew.

It was the best sex he ever had.

PART X

The Make-Believe Garden

45

Lord knows, that fire is a scary thing to them white folks, 'specially the ones that mean us harm. But it's good to have black people like Satchel and Galaxy. The colored folks that got the fire to fight back need to be down there sending them bad souls to the devil's place. But having that blue fire is a curse. Not the voodoo kind of roots you hear about in Louisiana, but the kind that sits heavy on the heart. 'Cause they know one day they gotta use it. Like Satchel did when that tiger came out of him. Mansa Musa didn't tell him that would happen because he wasn't supposed to know. But that's all right because black folks got good instincts. So, Satchel knowed exactly what to do when the tiger came out of him. That's why he sicced it on all them white folks who tried to kill him. Too bad he couldn't save his workers.

But at least he had another factory white people didn't know about. But that had nothing to do with Satchel's fire. It had to do with that mind he had. He knowed the best way to fight a thief was to hide stuff somewhere else. Thank the Lord he did, and thank King Mansa Musa for giving black men fire.

Mansa Musa done picked twelve black men to give the fire to every generation for hundreds of years. Only a few be alive at the same time. Every black man with fire got an animal in their soul, their spirit, waiting to come out and fight. But they can only use it once. Or, I better say it this way: It can only use them once. They have the fire for life, but that animal . . . Lord, it's a one-time thing. And that might be good because it take all the energy they got. If it happened more than once, they wouldn't have none left to live.

The thing is, people can see the fire animal when it's protecting them, but when it's over, the memory wash out they minds. The sparks do that to them. They 'member the safe life they get, but they don't 'member the fire that gave it to them. That's good because they would be calling Satchel and Galaxy and all the fire Negroes demons. People afraid of what they don't understand, so they have to call it something evil, even when it's good. Not all fire is dangerous. The fire that burns you is bad. The fire cooking the food that fill your belly is good.

Ain't no telling what Galaxy's fire animal is and when it gonna get a-loose. Poor Galaxy don't know either. But I know a little something nobody ever told him. An eagle landed on the windowsill of the hospital the day he was born, and it had blue fire coming out its eyes.

46

In 1935, a little girl in a pink-and-lavender dress journeyed down a dirt path with her book satchel strapped to her shoulders. Old math, English, and social studies books hindered her stride. She was used to the warm sun in Georgia, but there was something different about the sun in this place. It seemed closer, hotter, and more intimate. She tilted her head to the side so her bonnet could block the rays from striking her face.

Since everything back home had been close by, she wasn't accustomed to walking long distances. Taking a voyage to town just to buy sweet milk because the milkman didn't come to her house, or leaving home an hour early to make it to the schoolhouse on time was foreign to her. Navigating Mansaville seemed like a hassle for this young Georgian turned South Carolinian.

"Must be *some* church to bring us all the way here," she mumbled to herself as she passed by Liberty Baptist.

The church left her unimpressed. In her mind, the preaching wasn't good enough to make the whites from Sugarlake County stop calling her a nigger, nor was the choir good enough to sing her some new textbooks to put in the tattered satchel on her shoulder.

"Hey, wait a minute," a voice cried out.

The girl in the pink-and-lavender dress turned around and spotted another girl running out of a house.

"What's your name?"

"Sarah."

"Hi, Sarah. My name is Mary Anne." She caught her breath. "You're new here, right?"

"Yeah."

"Where are you from?" Mary Anne asked.

"Atlanta."

"Oh, I see. You got any friends?"

"Just my friends back home." Sarah stared at the ground. "Well, I guess this my home, but I can't talk right now. I gotta get back to start my chores." She put her head down and pressed on.

"I'll go with you. Since you don't have any friends here, I'll be your friend," Mary Anne said.

"Okay," Sarah responded as she angled her face to look at Mary Anne.

This brief conversation marked a turning point in both of their lives. They became true companions with a sisterly affection for one another. They would become inseparable. When one took sick, the other would watch over. On Sundays while in church, they would sit together and sing. When one forgot her Bible, the other would share, putting the Word between them and reading it together. As the years passed, they would eventually cover all thirty-nine of the Old Books and all twenty-seven of the New.

When they joined the youth choir and one would struggle to hit a note, the other would sing louder, as members of the congregation would shout, "All right now," and, "Take your time." They did exactly that—one with a raspy soulful voice, the other with a smooth angelic vibrato. They sang every hymn their hearts could muster, from "Amazing Grace" to their favorite, "Precious Lord."

At nineteen, Sarah's wedding wouldn't have been the same without Mary Anne helping her pick out the most spectacular dress, and years later, a widowed Sarah would arrange her husband's funeral with a little comfort because her matron of honor was there to help her select the finest casket: a brass-handled box with red lining and a cherry finish.

Mary Anne seldom witnessed Sarah cry, and seeing her do so after receiving word of her husband's death broke Mary Anne's heart. He had died in a car accident after losing control of his Ford when a heavy downpour clouded his vision. The car ran off of the road and into a tree that was older than him and Mansaville combined. Not able to defeat a stubborn pine, his car folded. The impact to his chest was too much to bear. He bled to death. The last things he saw were broken glass, blood, and wet kudzu vines. Not wanting to put her best friend through the turmoil of seeing his lukewarm, distorted corpse, Mary Anne felt obligated to identify the body.

She was also steadfast by Sarah's side when Sarah's brother, Blacky, died. His passing made life a lot more difficult for his little sister. But the Georgia native persevered until the end, raising the two Barkleys into manhood. The senior dead and the junior incarcerated, Sarah died without what she thought were her greatest accomplishments: her son, whom she raised as a single parent with little money, and her grandson, whom she fostered after his alcoholic mother abandoned him before he could say "Momma." Where Barkley's mother, Jewel, went, no one knew. She left without a trace. Grandma Jenkins couldn't remember a time when that woman was in her right mind.

Sarah only had one lengthy talk with Jewel, the young lady her son had been fooling around with for a year. Sarah remembered when the girl stumbled into the living room in a drunken daze. Jewel fell onto the slip-covered couch and attempted to speak clearly while rubbing her hair and twitching.

"Lord, have mercy on this poor child," Sarah said, shaking her head from side to side as she pieced together the intriguing tale the intoxicated woman told. She sat quietly as Jewel presented the story of the man with blue eyes who was the most beautiful angel in the City of Diamonds. His name was Tralamis. He wore the finest clothes—gold-trimmed robes with emeralds—and he had a flawless face that set the standard of beauty the brown-eyed angels both envied and admired.

Tralamis came to the city for a short stay, but his presence brought a lifetime of evil and destruction as dreadful as his robes were glamorous.

"What's beautiful ain't always pretty," Jewel said with a laugh that sounded more like a gasp.

Who caused the city's destruction? Was it Tralamis, or was it the people who hated him? Before Grandma Jenkins was given the answer, Jewel had left the county with the swiftness of the blue-eyed angel. That was the last Sarah saw of her, and she was glad to see Jewel and her alcohol leave town, taking the woman's departure as an opportunity to raise Barkley Jr. as best she could with her limited money and unlimited conviction. Though Jewel wasn't there anymore, her story stayed with Sarah and haunted her for years. The only person with whom Sarah shared the tale was Mary Anne, a superstitious individual who let it torment her even more.

Years later, when Sarah was on her deathbed, it was her faith and Mary Anne keeping her alive for a few more days. Sarah had no regrets about her negative experiences: family members' early deaths, abandonment, relatives in prison, poverty, poor formal education, hot treks home. She simply had prayers, one of which was for Barkley Jr. to be by her side, clutching her hand as Death and Mary Anne argued over who got to hold the other.

As Sarah took her last breath, she closed her eyes to pray, opened them to see her childhood friend, then shut them again, forever. She and Mary Anne had taken comfort in holding each other's hands. Spiritually, Sarah had graduated from relying on the church. By the time of her passing, she had only needed God and thanked Him for having put her best friend by her side. Mary Anne may have had her issues, but she understood this very thing: If you give loved ones flowers when they are alive, you won't have to put any by their tombstones after they die.

47

All of the businesses were closed the day after the church burned down. The boss man at the factory even gave his employees the day off. That had never happened before. People who were old enough recalled when the church was first built and how it gave the town a spark of life. It was as though they had lost a close relative whom they would mourn for years to come.

An elderly lady with emphysema lay dying in the hospital, wishing she could worship at the church one more time before going to Glory, oblivious to the building's destruction. "Y'all know I want my funeral to be held at Liberty Baptist. I want to be buried out back just like my husband James." Her son didn't have the heart to tell her the news, so he just grabbed her hand and said, "Okay, Momma . . . okay," as he wept at her bedside.

The factory side's residents were devastated.

"Lord, have mercy. Somebody done burned down the church."

"I bet it was some of them white folks. I knew they were gonna get us sooner or later."

"They always do."

"God knows, that church is our beacon of hope."

"You mean it *was* our beacon of hope."

"Jesus, help this town."

"And heaven help the soul who did this."

"You right about that. They the ones need help, not us."

"You know they having a vigil tonight?"

"Yep, I'm going to be there. So is my whole family."

"Mine, too."

"Deacon Jones been calling around telling everybody they need to come."

"Nobody got calls from Reverend Whitaker?"

"He probably beside himself. That church was all he had."

"He got Mary Anne."

"That church was all he had."

The wild laughter they let out ended upon the realization that they were wrong for cracking jokes during such serious times. This was one of the few instances when laughter could slow down the healing process. The two walked down the street in complete silence as they reminisced about all of the good things that had happened in that sacred building. They thought about the singing that was so powerful it could be heard beyond the doors. The time when Liberty Baptist was remodeled with money raised by fish fries and car washes. The Sundays when they would go to church and stand around and talk until nightfall. The graduation cookouts for their sons and daughters and grandsons and granddaughters. They had a lot of good times at Liberty Baptist Church, but if they had known about all of the butt-fucking that had gone on there, them niggas would've burned it down themselves.

48

The clouds lingered and cast a blanket of darkness that erased people's shadows as they walked the streets. Even the birds retreated, and the grass in the playground seemed a bit flat. When Barkley awoke, dimness still loomed in the air. He assumed summer rain was about to shower the community, wishing it would so he could postpone his normal activities to spend time with Galaxy. A day with no outside visitors was what he needed most.

Mary Anne's abrupt exit from church the other day had weighed little on their minds because the reverend cleaned up the debris from Mary Anne's trainwreck with a barn burner of a sermon. Despite her display, Galaxy and Barkley had been pleased with the service. It was everything Barkley had hoped it would be and everything Galaxy had imagined. To his own surprise, Galaxy had even engaged in generic banter with a few members of the congregation as Barkley wandered off to start his own conversations, smiling at his boyfriend from across the room. Though they didn't show too much affection for one another, they had walked a little closer on the way home. For once, they had spent the whole day together, and when the horizon drowned the sun, the two had cuddled each other to sleep. But that seemed so long ago as they now lay in bed after another night of nestling.

"You awake?" Barkley asked shortly after sunrise.

"Yeah, I was up early, but I decided to stay here and watch you sleep," Galaxy said.

"I think it would've been better if you was in the kitchen fixing me something to eat."

Galaxy smiled.

"Don't worry about cooking, little man. Just keep laying on your king's chest."

Galaxy did exactly that and enjoyed the warmth against his face as he closed his eyes and went to sleep again. Barkley held him and listened to the harmonious sound of Galaxy's breath. They felt good to one another.

Galaxy awoke when Barkley got up to answer the door. When he opened it, Paul was standing there with sweat running down his forehead.

"What's up? Is the police after us?" Barkley asked.

"No," Paul said before crossing the threshold and explaining that somebody had burned down the church. While speaking, he shook his head and looked at the floor.

"Galaxy, come out here!" Barkley said.

This was one of the rare times Barkley acknowledged Galaxy's presence when someone else was in the house, and Galaxy appreciated the acceptance it gave him. He retrieved his brush and stroked his hair while standing in front of a looking glass. He then picked up a bottle of women's perfume and squirted a little on his neck. Not bothering to put on pants and a shirt, he strutted into the living room wearing a pair of white briefs.

Paul flashed a warm smile. He hugged Galaxy, who stood there with his arms around the other man's neck, and Paul wrapped his arms around the lower portion of Galaxy's back while taking in the sweet smell of perfume. All three men beamed.

"What's wrong?" Galaxy asked.

"Somebody burned down the church," Paul replied.

"Is it gone completely?" Galaxy asked.

"Yeah, man. Ain't nothing there but the front stairs and a pile of ashes." Paul regarded Galaxy's face and forced himself not to gaze at his body.

"Why would somebody do that?" Galaxy asked.

"Take one guess," Paul stole a glance at Galaxy's chest and stomach.

"My grandma used to tell me something like this was going to happen one day," Barkley added.

"She was right. I always thought she knew everything," Paul said to Barkley while looking at Galaxy.

"She did. If she was alive, this would've been what killed her. Liberty Baptist was her second home," Barkley said.

Galaxy had never witnessed his boyfriend behave with this kind of sensitivity.

"Where's the reverend?" Barkley asked.

"Nobody's heard from him. They say he had a nervous breakdown after he heard the news, but I don't know how true that is." Paul's voice had begun to slow down.

"It probably ain't true. You know how rumors get started." Barkley's voice had been steady the whole time.

"There's supposed to be a vigil tonight. Me and Tyrone are going, and y'all should come, too. It'll be at the church, or what's left of it."

"I'll be there for my grandmother."

"I'll come, too," Galaxy said.

"All right. See y'all later. It starts at seven," Paul said.

"Okay, man. Later." Barkley grabbed Paul's hand and pulled him in for a partial hug. Paul then gave Galaxy a kiss on the cheek.

"I'll see you there tonight, little man."

Galaxy nodded his head and watched Paul leave the house.

Although Galaxy had only been to the church a few times (mainly for funerals), he felt a deep connection to it, as if he had been baptized there, as if his grandmother had dragged him there every Sunday. He had a sense of emptiness borne out in his desire to be a part of this culture, something the Goodfellows lacked because all they had was money.

"Are you okay, sugar?"

"Yeah. I'm just thinking about how I used to skip church and how I always got mad when Grandma asked me to go." Barkley blinked to hold back tears as he sat down on the couch.

Galaxy took a spot next to him and leaned on his king's broad shoulder. Barkley kissed the top of Galaxy's head.

"Thanks, little man."

They listened to the rain, its drops pattering on the windowsill in a desolate song that overpowered the sounds of their breathing. When the music stopped, Galaxy stood up, drifted to the window, and peered at the Almighty's tears, which hopped on the surface of the ground before settling into puddles.

In the house across the street, a woman cried as well—weeping Mary Anne—wife of the man who did this, mother of the baby who cried blood.

All the while, Liberty Baptist was gone, for there had been no tears to put out the reverend and the devil's flames. That's why the sky cried as well . . . only too late to save the church.

49

On the evening of the vigil, it seemed as if every resident of the factory side stood on the church grounds with watery eyes. They stared at the ashes where pews and green carpet used to be. The mural of Mary holding her Son was a mere memory, as were the windows that were now pieces of broken glass glimmering in the ashes. The only sounds were feet hitting the gravel as people of all ages trekked the winding road. Tears, embraces, and kisses on cheeks replaced preaching, singing, and tithing. No one saw oddity in how Galaxy and Barkley were holding hands, nor did they care that one of them was a Goodfellow. Galaxy's attendance comforted them, as did the presence of every soul gathered at the site of what was once the best church in the South.

Just down the road in a little yellow house with a covered porch, Mary Anne walked to her closet to locate her finest attire: a blue pantsuit and a crisp white blouse. She had bought the outfit the previous year with money her husband had given her fresh from the collection plate, but until this day, she had never found an occasion fitting to sport such extravagant clothing. Today Mary Anne would deck it out with a timeless pair of black pumps she'd bought years back (though they'd never been worn either) and the teardrop diamond earrings that had dangled from her ears at her best friend's funeral. Mary Anne had put them in a box that had since collected dust.

Back at the church grounds, residents of the factory side held hands.

"We shall overcome," sang the deacon in a soulful voice as everyone joined in.

Not knowing the words, Galaxy stood there in awe of their resolve and faith. Their church had burned down; the place where they married, christened their children, and worshipped was destroyed. What, he wondered, would happen to this side of Mansaville now? That gem of a church had anchored it. The barbershop, the schoolhouses, the Christmas parades, Leroy's Corner Store—all came *after* the church.

Having stayed behind to cook while her husband left to prepare for the service, a seventy-six-year-old woman in a shabby housedress hobbled down the winding road. She had stopped baking her Bundt cake upon remembering the vigil was about to start. Before making it to the crowd, she was already singing. As the spiritual ended, she broke into the circle of people and reached for Galaxy's hand. He leaned over and whispered, "Hi, Mrs. Jones." Betty Mae returned a warm, approving smile.

All extraneous pain was put aside for now. For once, there was just pure harmony. They sang and cried as one. Galaxy, Barkley, Paul, and Deacon Jones were the only men who fought back tears.

"Precious Lord, take my hand," a man sang, signaling that the first rendition hadn't been enough. As if on cue, everyone backed him, "Lead me on, let me stand." Without a clear pattern, there was more singing and prayer as the townspeople held the service. The pain in their voices made the hymn echo, although they stood on open ground with trees that were too far away to matter, except Mister Tree.

Just down yonder in a little yellow house, Mary Anne was dressed for the vigil. After gathering her clutch purse and the keys to her Buick, she went back to her closet and fumbled around the top shelf to retrieve one more thing.

Back at the site, the vigil continued. It drizzled. Raindrops tickled the heads of the townspeople as they fellowshipped.

"We're going to have one last prayer before we go back home to be with our families and move on with our lives." The deacon wiped rain from his eye, lest somebody reckon he was crying. With dull gray cloaking the sky, no one noticed. "This is not a sad day for Mansaville.

This is a day of hope. This is a day of worship. There's nothing sad about praising God, church or no church. They can burn down the steeple, and they can burn down every pew, but they can't burn down the foundation."

People yelled "Hallelujah" and "Well, well" as the precipitation picked up, a poignant accessory to the deacon's prayer. "We know bad times come, O Lord, but in the name of Jesus, bad times will go."

The sun, tired of being hidden by clouds, descended as the sound of a car motor interrupted the prayer. Barkley stood on the concrete stairs as the headlights shone across his back. He turned to see what had stolen everyone's attention. Galaxy recognized the vehicle and recalled Mary Anne's evil stares as she had observed him go in and out of Sarah Jenkins's old house.

"Mary Anne know she wrong for coming to the service all late," Betty Mae said to herself as the sedan's lights made her squint.

Mary Anne maneuvered the car along the winding road. Outraged at her attempt to make a grand entrance, the townspeople and Galaxy watched without speaking. The car door swung open, and Mary Anne's left foot made contact with the dirt, then her right foot. She emerged to reveal her striking blue-and-white outfit to everyone. Appalled, people shook their heads—even Galaxy. The nonconformists were Ray, whose emotion was anger, and Betty Mae, who was embarrassed by her close friend's display.

Betty Mae broke away from the crowd and approached her. Sensing the vigil was over, the others began to journey home. Some made eye contact with Mary Anne while still shaking their heads; others tried not to look at her, not wanting to give her the attention she craved. Betty Mae stood close to Mary Anne, who had paced around to the passenger side to open the door.

"Child, what is your problem?" Betty Mae asked.

"Nothing, girl, I'm just about to rid this place of sin." Mary Anne pointed toward the concrete stairs in front of what used to be an entrance.

"Girl, what are you talking about?" Betty Mae asked.

"I'm talking 'bout that blue-eyed Goodfellow boy."

"He ain't got no blue eyes, girl."

"Yes, he do. I saw them plain." Mary Anne pointed. "That's Tralamis."

"Who?"

"He's the blue-eyed Angel of Death, and I know it."

Mary Anne leaned into the car, pulled out a shotgun, and waved it around with both hands.

"Oh, Lord, you done gone over fool's hill!" Betty Mae placed her hands on her head.

"I'm gonna kill him!"

"No, don't kill him! That little boy ain't done nothing to you!" Betty Mae said.

"No, I can't shoot the Angel of Death. I gotta kill what's most important to him. You can't kill the blue-eyed devil," Mary Anne said while cocking the gun.

Everyone's eyes widened. They were so concerned about the gun they ignored her words. With their bodies, husbands shielded their wives. Barkley positioned himself in front of Galaxy. Parents slung their crying children behind them. Terror jam-packed the air.

"What done got into you, girl?" With her rain-dampened clothes clinging to her, Betty Mae pulled the fabric from her skin with pinched fingers.

Knowing he and Johnny had caused Mary Anne so much harm over the years, Ray feared the rifle more than anyone, thinking he was its prime target. Believing she had immunity from any gunfire, Betty Mae wasn't afraid.

While holding the shotgun, Mary Anne thought of Barkley's baptism. She had smiled as her best friend's grandson, wearing a long white christening gown, was dipped into the waters of the large tin tub, and she and her friend had wept together. Mary Anne once treasured Barkley for the joy he brought, and to this day, his baptism was the best birthday present she had ever received. Way back then, she adored him more than any other child in the world.

Even before Sarah died, Mary Anne felt the need to take care of him. Every May when he was a child, Barkley would go to the store to buy some glue, markers, glitter, and construction paper, and the following Sunday, Mary Anne would smile when she received the poorly crafted Mother's Day card. She returned the favor every year by giving him a wrinkled bill on his birthday and would later write him a check for twenty-five dollars to open his first account at Emancipation Bank.

But that was a long time ago.

Now, she detested Barkley for what she believed to be disrespect for her best friend. "If Sarah was alive and saw what that child was doing . . ." she would mumble to herself upon seeing Barkley and Galaxy—an incomplete sentence she was about to finish.

Mary Anne wanted to honor the memory of her friend by righting the "wrongs" of anyone who soiled her grave. She thought for years about the story Sarah told her and came up with her own ending. The way to defeat Tralamis was by piercing his blue eyes and therefore destroying what distinguished him from everyone else. What made Galaxy different from most men in Mansaville? He had a boyfriend.

She aimed the gun at Barkley, who froze in fear. This was the first time Galaxy saw Barkley as physically vulnerable, and he could do nothing to help.

"Don't shoot him!" shouted Betty Mae.

With her shotgun aimed and cocked, Mary Anne wended her way toward Barkley.

She fired the gun.

Barkley fell.

Many in the crowd screamed. Some ran.

Two men tackled her as a third confiscated the rifle. Mary Anne Whitaker resigned without a struggle, although she pursed her lips and said, "Y'all niggas fucking up my suit."

Betty Mae now towered over Mary Anne. "Girl, what have you done?"

"I did the right thing. I know I did." Mary Anne spoke in a low yet confident voice.

"How could you do such a thing?" Betty Mae asked with tears in her eyes. "You ain't done nobody no good. Nobody!" The deacon's spouse blinked to release more tears.

"I stopped Tralamis from destroying Mansaville."

A few feet away, Galaxy knelt as he held Barkley's head in his lap. Barkley lay there with blood seeping from his chest.

"Somebody call an ambulance!" Galaxy found the voice to cry out.

Everyone stood there hovering over the wounded ex-convict, who angled his eyes toward Mary Anne. By then she was standing up and looking at him. Barkley gazed at her as his vision clouded over with waters of sadness.

"I loved you like a mother, Mrs. Whitaker," Barkley said as he coughed up blood.

His words impaled her like the bullet that had pierced him. For a moment guilt overwhelmed Mary Anne as she registered the devastation on her former godson's face. The sight of blood exiting Barkley's chest muted Galaxy, who knelt at his boyfriend's side and stroked his dark hair. Believing Barkley would always be around, Galaxy had pictured the two of them living together forever in the quaint house on Church Street.

With Galaxy there holding him, Barkley was numb to the gunshot wound. The last feeling he had in life was the touch of Galaxy's hand across the top of his head. He could not have perished to a better caress. At that moment, Barkley Jenkins Jr. took a breath and flew away like loose pages of Exodus in the wind.

On one of those floating pages, the Eighth Commandment forbids you from stealing, but it's okay to steal away to be with the Lord. And that's what Barkley did. Prior to expiring, he drew from his grandmother's pool of parlance and whispered, "I reckon this is my time, Sweet Jesus. I'm walking yonder way to my mansion up high." His body took on eternal stillness—like the waters of Galilee—waters whose reflection beckoned him to look at Sarah's face shimmering in the water right before he passed on to his reward. Like most, he wasn't given a choice of how to die. That decision had been rendered by society's gun, for in his head rested the conjugating bullet that had turned the tense of his life from present to past.

Why the hell did Mary Anne take Barkley's life? It was one of the things Confederate skeletons liked most: blacks snuffing each other out. Her killing of Barkley marked the first time in the history of Mansaville that a black person murdered another. The townspeople failed to understand the gravity of it all, so Mister Tree—the mostly silent oak—howled, scaring everyone in the vicinity of the once-vibrant Liberty Baptist Church. Mister Tree sang in a hollow voice: *"Them skeletons gonna ride they horses. They gonna get they swords and kill everybody."*

The clouds congregated as if they were sitting in sky-high pews. Thunder came. Then lightning. Thick blood rained from the sky.

"Oh, Lord. The war is beginning," a woman said as the devil's tears stained her dress in blood. "Mary Anne, what have you done?"

The tree howled so loudly it could be heard in the industrial district on the other side of the body of water that now boiled. Having grown to the size of a toddler, Old Scratch stood on a wooden raft floating on the haunted river from which skeletons were emerging.

There were so many of them!

Bones of the Confederate soldiers crawled out of the river. They mounted horses whose flesh was still intact.

Old Scratch rubbed the scar on his eye and said, "Now's the time."

With the words of a demon child, an entire army of skeletons on horseback rose from the river. The stallions—scores of them—galloped toward the grounds of the burned-down Liberty Baptist Church. The rumble of their bloody hooves sounded like thunder but felt like an earthquake.

Mister Tree continued to howl as the Confederates approached.

Old Scratch, however, stayed on the river that had now risen, releasing the smell of death.

"Them skeletons gonna ride they horses. They gonna get they swords and kill everybody."

The rumbles boomed, briefly drowning out the tree's song. Some of the townspeople prayed. Others ran with blood soaking their clothes, but they didn't get far. When they caught sight of the army and lightning striking the terrain, they turned around and ran back to the church grounds.

"Them skeletons gonna ride they horses. They gonna get they swords and kill everybody."

The pungent smell impurified the air as the wind from the storm brought the odor close, making Mister Tree's branches sway.

"We all gonna die."

"Jesus, help us."

"Protect us, O Lord."

The thunder coming from the sky was as loud as the noise of the hooves as the army advanced close enough for the vigil-goers to see.

"They got swords!"

"Yes, they do. Mister Tree was right."

As the army approached, Galaxy's back tingled. The sensation turned into burning pain, forcing him to the ground. When the townspeople swarmed around him, he rolled over on his stomach, the side of his face touching the dirt. It was as if a gust had ripped Galaxy's shirt from his body. His back gleamed while he moaned in agony.

"Lord, what's happening to that poor boy?" a woman cried out.

"He's the Protector," her husband said with tears running down his face.

No one else spoke, out of crippling horror. They simply raised their hands to the sky.

"Them skeletons gonna ride they horses. They gonna get they swords and kill everybody."

A burst of blue shot out of Galaxy's back as a firebird slowly rose from his dark skin. The eagle of blue fire grew, sending cobalt flames outward, forcing the townspeople to step away. The firebird surged, its flames growing hotter, its light becoming brighter. It detached from Galaxy's back and ascended to the sky, opening its beak to let out the powerful sound of a siren; all the while, blue flames continued to scatter from its wings.

The siren could be heard all over town. Everyone in Mansaville went outside and looked to the heavens to see the firebird gracefully moving its wings, casting a glorious spell of heat across the land. Not a single person stayed indoors.

The firebird's beak closed.

The siren hushed.

Mister Tree stopped chanting.

Silence.

Then came birds, flapping their wings in a frenzy in preparation for their singsong. They came from their perch on Mister Tree, except there were more of them than the tree could possibly hold. The birds littered the sky, unafraid of the sapphire.

Some call them whip-o-wills, but you might call them nightjars. Either way, they circled the sky above the skeleton army, and like only a flock of nightjars could, they sang—not to you, not to anyone you know, but to the eagle. Yes, the blue firebird that had emerged from Galaxy's body in a blaze of splendor.

The sapphire firebird spread its wings, killing the silence with a whistling draft of warm wind. The townspeople, including those below the firebird, fell to their knees and spread their arms in praise. Then came the fire—the blue blazes that flew from its wings hurled spheres of flames at the skeletons and hit the one closest to Barkley's dead body. The skeleton, its skull consumed with blue fire, ran around in a circle and wailed. The fire worked its way down the spine and rib cage and eventually engulfed every bone. The skeleton's screams grew higher in pitch and more fervent, only to stop when all of its bones burst, emitting blue sparks that would vanish. Within minutes, every skeleton possessed a skull of blue fire. They all hollered and ran around, some torn asunder while standing, the weaker ones falling to the ground before succumbing to the sapphire flames.

A wail.
A singsong from the nightjars.
A howling tree.
Running skeletons.
Another wail.
White supremacy be damned,
for the Blue Eagle has arisen!

Miles away, Old Scratch fell off of his raft and into the boiling river. He shrieked.

"Mommy, help me." The blood in the river had never been this hot. Old Scratch, still a toddler, winced.

The remaining skeletons heard his cry and retreated, causing the thunderous sound of hooves to become louder, only to disappear into silence as they made their way back to the Confederate River. The skeletons—at least the ones that had not been re-killed with sapphire flames—crept toward the body of water and submerged themselves in its bloody current, wading, not swimming, and eventually sinking into the river that was no longer boiling. You could still detect the odor of death, but now it smelled like the corpses of Confederates and not just the remains of slaves. Some of the skulls floated on top of the river, and their mouths were open as if they had been screaming right before they perished for the second (or even third) time.

Back yonder on the church grounds by Barkley's dead body, Mary Anne's breasts bled before shrinking to the size they were before they produced the blood that had nurtured Old Scratch. She clutched her bosom while thrashing about and letting out a scream of her own.

"I can't feed my baby no more," Mary Anne yelled as she looked at the thick blood covering her expensive garments, Confederate gore that came from a black woman's bosom. Her outfit was once just blue and white, but now—spangled with blood—it was red, white, and blue. With her own actions, Mary Anne had fed the same racism that sought to destroy her, and now she literally had blood on her hands. She stuck her ring finger into her mouth to have a taste. She recoiled as a sting filled her throat.

"Lord, this is what I've been feeding my baby?" Mary Anne asked while looking down at the rifle she had used to murder her former godson. The shotgun somehow remained unscathed, shining brilliantly without a single drop of blood on it, not even from the breast of the monster that had just wielded it. Still being restrained by two men, she looked up and closed her eyes. The sapphire flames were too bright for her.

As Mary Anne fell to her knees, Mister Tree howled. Everyone looked in its direction except Galaxy, who was on the ground staring at the miraculous eagle that had materialized from his back. Mister Tree sang:

"Souls will be free.
Slave spirits will fly.
Go be with the Lord.
Take your place in the sky."

How could such a monstrous tree sing so beautifully?

The townspeople held hands and joined in, repeating its song. Mister Tree trembled, his leaves rustling to make the sound of tambourines whose metal clanged in rhythm, causing some of the people to clap in unison. The souls' orange lights glimmered on the branches of the tree. Each glow took the faint shape of a slave who had been hanged there. Dozens and dozens of humanlike lights soared into the heavens past the firebird that freed them. Like Mister Tree's lyrics once decreed, they took their place in the sky. Had you not seen them leave this world with your own eyes, you would have thought they were stars in the night sky. And yes, each one was a star, but not the kind that was light-years away.

"The souls are free now.
Seeds of freedom are sown.
They're resting with the Lord.
They done gone home."

That was Mister Tree's call. The sapphire firebird's response was to take on an elegant posture as it flapped its sweltering wings while descending toward the church grounds. Everyone stared as it flew behind what remained of the church and landed near the mighty oak. While the townspeople looked on in silence, the sapphire eagle wrapped its wings around Mister Tree, engulfing him in blue flames. The firebird burst before disappearing, leaving the burning tree shining majestically in the conflagration.

As the whip-o-wills stopped singing and dispersed, the townspeople saw a sight—a truly awful one: the naked body of Reverend Whitaker hanging by a rope from a branch of the tree. From the front, they couldn't see the knife in his corpse's back.

The reverend's lifeless body gazed at his widow.

Mary Anne stared back.

The first true eye contact they had made since exchanging vows—too bad one of them was dead. When the eye contact broke, so did her heart.

"Forgive me, everyone," his remains, crestfallen in spades, spoke before being consumed by flames.

The blue fire burned flesh and entrails but spared rope and bones, leaving nothing but a skeleton hanging from Mister Tree. For this, Mary Anne was grateful, for she would rather lose her marriage by death than by divorce because the latter would have been seen as her own failure.

"Thank you, Johnny," the newly minted murderer whispered.

With those words, Mary Anne thought of her make-believe garden, the one she had nurtured behind her broken home. She remembered the countless hours spent planting seeds of nothingness while hoping something wonderful would sprout. But only weeds inhabited her backyard because imaginary fertilizer never makes flowers grow.

50

As Mary Anne rode in the back of the police car, Old Scratch, a toddler with tears of blood flowing from his eyes, sat next to her.

"I hear a baby crying," the police officer said.

Mary Anne smiled and said, "He's my little devil child."

Chalking it up to Mrs. Whitaker's madness, the police officer didn't respond.

Old Scratch stopped weeping and giggled as a snake slithered from his right eye. It was a five-foot-long serpent, black with a red stripe going down its back. Mary Anne tried to scream, but the snake had already attached itself to her face, covering her mouth and coiling around her neck. Old Scratch snickered again as a spider crawled out of his throat, onto his tongue, and out of his mouth. The furry arachnid was the size of Mary Anne's hand. It had a large, dark-gray abdomen that also bore a blood-colored stripe. The spider's legs made the clamor of metal clanging against metal as it moved across the back seat and climbed Mary Anne's left thigh. She tried to yell once more, but the snake silenced her, affording the spider a background of hush as the metallic-sounding legs produced a rhythm with each motion up Mary Anne's torso. The arachnid rested on her bosom before using its legs to cut a slit in Mary Anne's skin just outside of her heart and rib cage. It crawled in and made its way through her ribs, the gash closing and healing in seconds. The spider spread its limbs around her heart and squeezed until the beating stopped. Mary Anne closed her eyes as the snake loosened its grip around her mouth and neck. The serpent shrank and returned to its resting place inside the devilish eye of her only begotten son.

Old Scratch looked at her dead body and laughed wildly because it was the most amusing slaughter he'd ever orchestrated. The same daggercidal demon baby who had just murdered Mary Anne was the same child who had been killing her all along. Despite having accumulated so many expensive things over the course of her existence, she had failed to realize that dignity was life's most valuable trophy of prosperity. Lacking understanding and drowning in spiritual bankruptcy, Mary Anne had possessed fur coats, high-end jewelry, and a solvent bank account, but she still died a broke-ass bitch.

51

Betty Mae, the new first lady of Liberty Baptist Church, would go next door to sit on the porch by an empty chair, talking to a friend who was no longer around and gossiping about a couple of men across the street who weren't there anymore. Her husband stood at the window and watched her converse with the air, and he openly cried for the first time in months. Ray had never wept in front of others, but now the tears poured freely because he didn't slide any concern toward other people's opinions anymore. He was tired.

He had surprised himself by not crying when he saw Johnny's dead body swinging from the tree. Ray was angry that the reverend had abandoned him without so much as a note. He hoped his own predisposition had died with Johnny, allowing him to be the husband Betty Mae deserved. His wife, though depressed over recent events, had the marriage she always wanted, however phony it was.

Perhaps most telling of all was that no one mourned the death of their reverend, not even the elderly members who thought he did no wrong. Their sole worry was finding someone else to lead them, and Ray accepted the challenge. Most reckoned he would do a better job than Johnny, though no one voiced their opinions. Despite what they may have thought about the late reverend, they never spoke ill of the dead. Instead, they would pray for his soul, one they rightly assumed had been banished to the underworld.

Johnny Whitaker belonged down there. His spirit had lacked the strength to open the doors to Eternal Salvation because the gates to heaven are the heaviest of them all. It's the doors to hell that are the easiest to open.

52

Although the building was gone, Liberty Baptist Church pressed on. Its members convened in the once-empty space above the barbershop. They left their finest Sunday clothes at home and came as they were. The praise remained the same, and the choir could still sing the Holy Ghost into the small, overcrowded room, where some members had to stand and lean against the wall. And people always caught the Ghost when It came. Some even looked back at the doorway thinking Galaxy would walk through, but he never did.

Another door had opened for Galaxy. For once in his life, he felt understood. Those people must have accepted that the love was real when they saw him weeping after Barkley was gunned down. They had to know the relationship was genuine as they stood around and cried as much for Galaxy as they did for the loss of one of their own.

On the night of Barkley's slaying, Galaxy had hurried back to the house, not even waiting for the body to be taken away. He knew he would leave the factory side of Mansaville before Barkley's remains were cold, before the fierce winds dried the rain and blood-soaked ground. Realizing his stay had come to an end, he had to run from the pain, escape from being in a house all alone, and get away from the inquiries and pity from the residents of a town where everybody nodded at each other and waved at passing cars.

Once away from the church grounds and out of everyone's view, he ran as fast as his body would allow. He didn't have a reason to stay, nor did he possess the motivation to wait and answer questions from the law. (His responses weren't needed anyway since there were dozens of witnesses to Mary Anne's crime.) Galaxy's focus was on the passing of Barkley and the death of the firebird that had emerged from his back. He and Old Scratch would be the only ones who would remember what happened that day. The townspeople would be able to recall the skeletons, the horses, and, of course, the whip-o-wills but not the blue flames that saved them. They would all go on believing that the song of the nightjars and the chant from Mister Tree destroyed the Confederate army. And naturally, they would also assign their safety to a collective prayer they had sent up to the heavens. But Galaxy knew what had transpired and tried to process his powers. The fire that had made him feel so different and alone was now the fire he wanted to keep.

When Galaxy entered the house for what would be the last time, he cried, realizing this was the first night he would spend without the comfort of knowing Barkley would return. Some evenings, Barkley would leave to take care of his illegal business affairs, but he always came home to cuddle Galaxy into slumber.

Scarcely able to see for the tears in his eyes, Galaxy trudged to the kitchen to get a drink of water. His emotions wouldn't permit hunger, so all he had to quell was his thirst. He took two mason jars out of the cabinet, rinsed them out, and filled them with ice. He spotted a magnet hanging on the refrigerator. Displayed on it was a copy of the Ten Commandments.

Barkley was never a religious man, but he had posted the Commandments in a conspicuous place to pay his respects to his late grandmother, who always urged him to keep them on hand. Galaxy read them all, but one—Exodus 20:12—stuck with him: "Honor thy father and thy mother: that thy days may be long upon the land which the Lord God giveth thee." Barkley had failed to honor his parents: one, whose life he once thought he took, and the other, whom he had called out of her name more than he called her "Momma."

Crackling sounds persisted as water smothered ice cubes in the containers Galaxy placed on the table. One jar for him, the other for

Barkley. At the end of the sitting, Barkley's jar was full; Galaxy's was empty. He sat there for over an hour, crying while staring at the full vessel of water, wishing his boyfriend would come home to drink.

He ushered himself to the sleeping quarters to experience one more night in a bed dressed in sheets still carrying Barkley's loving fragrance. Starved of his boyfriend's presence, the bed was as cold and hollow as a cave. With his face treasuring the pillow's touch, Galaxy closed his eyes to overwinter, though the season called for sleep.

෬෩

Before the sun dismissed the moon, Galaxy got in his car to begin his departure from the factory side of town. He was leaving a place whose core had been decimated. People would wonder if their oasis could survive without Liberty Baptist Church, this side of Mansaville's spiritual reason for being.

The town is resilient, some thought.

No, it's just going to crumble, others believed.

Galaxy, however, knew both sides of Mansaville would survive. He also understood that he would remain standing despite the hard times that had come and those that could return. What had become important to him was Barkley's legacy and all of the memories this place had given him, even the unpleasant ones.

As he turned out of the driveway, a sense of accomplishment filled him for having lived on his own without his mother. Galaxy didn't mind the water on the ground that lingered from the previous day's rain. His newfound ability to endure life did away with minor inconveniences like wet roads and muddy tires and damp leaves caught in windshield wipers, and even the bits of grass that stuck to the sides of his shoes.

Galaxy knew going back to live at his family's estate wouldn't be so unbearable after all because he now had the courage to leave again if the need arose. Besides, he would soon be back at Morehouse College, the place where fire rituals took place. Galaxy decided against returning to the factory side of town for Barkley's funeral. He knew Barkley's spirit wanted him to move on.

As he drove away, Galaxy avoided glancing in the rearview mirror to see the home get smaller in the distance. It didn't matter anyway because the house would still be around, nestled right there on Church Street with the door unlocked as he had left it. The cozy little domicile would sit quietly, collecting dust on the inside, waiting for someone else to enter to create lasting memories.

Galaxy kept driving, fighting the urge to go back to the ashen place where Liberty Baptist Church once stood. He halted when a white cat ran out into the middle of the road. Unafraid and beautiful, the feline had a coat of fur resembling the purest cloud ever to drift over Mansaville. Galaxy wasn't bothered and didn't consider maneuvering his car around it because he was in no real hurry. So, he waited for the cat as it peered through the windshield at him, who interpreted the slight movement of its mouth as a grin. It walked across the road, only to get lost behind the wild grass and trees that were moist with morning dew. Galaxy smiled until he thought about the Order of Black Dragons. The secret society had been on his mind ever since his mother mentioned its name. Yearning to understand what it all meant, he was eager to get home to talk to her, believing she would be there to tell him all he needed to know.

But he was wrong.

When Galaxy would arrive at his home, he would find the dead bodies of his mother and little sister lying face down on the living room floor. Each corpse would have a knife in its back. Next to his murdered kindred, Galaxy would see footprints of blood leading to the threshold of his now haunted house. The bloody footprints would be oh-so small because they were those of a three-thousand-year-old toddler named Old Scratch.

But now, Galaxy was leaving Barkley and Grandma Sarah's

side of Mansaville. He looked to his right and saw the sign that read "Confederate River." Galaxy took a deep breath, filling his lungs with air that was thin and easy to breathe. Then, with a sense of calm he'd never had before, he took his right foot off of the brake, causing the vehicle to roll back slightly, eased his left foot off of the clutch, and pressed the gas pedal.

With tears in his eyes, he wondered what Barkley had been thinking when he took his last breath. Galaxy would have been pleased to know the truth. Barkley had thought of a conversation he once had with his grandmother, who was now up yonder waiting for him to come home.

Sit down, sugar
Let me talk to you
You're my grandson
That's why I made you that sweet potato pie last week

You know, baby, the Glory Train is gonna get me one day
So, I wanna tell you something I ain't never told you
I know you're different than other boys

But the Good Lord loves you
He made you the way He wanted you to be

So, don't waste strength fighting those devils coming out of the darkness
Sometimes you don't have to punch back
Just be still like the waters of Galilee
The stillness will hit them harder than your fist

When you used to fall, I retch down and picked you up
And you always got up better than you was before you fell

'Cause God gave you that inside strength
Them folks know it and can't stand it
They think they love is the only kind

Love ain't something you can just whip up like Sunday dinner
The Lord puts it in you—
And He puts it on the heart side of your chest

Now, I'm about to make you a mess of okra, a mess of fried chicken,
Some biscuits, and that good ol' cream corn
While I'm cooking, be still, sugar

And look out the window at the beautiful rainbow the Good Lord put
in the sky.